This fictional story's origin is purely that of the writer's imagination. Therefore, any and/or resemblance of actual people to these characters, themes, and/or plots are entirely coincidental and should be regarded as such.

Also, By Luna Charles

Men Are Not The Problem

- Vol I

MAKTUB Trust Group

Presents

Men Are Not The Problem

VOL II

Luna Charles

Table of Contents

Part 2 6

Chapter X 8

Chapter XI 29

Chapter XII 69

Chapter XIII 84

Chapter XIV 89

Chapter XV 103

Chapter XVI 122

Chapter XVII 131

Chapter XVIII 157

Chapter XIX 172

Part 2

(Fear, Action & Consequence ...)

Fear was all I knew, so I stayed trapped
in my own life.
Too scared to move on to something new.
Afraid to face what I did not know, that
any new place was worse than what I had
learned.
Love, hope, happiness, and courage had
all left me alone in fear.
In the distance, down the road, I saw the
shadows of what might be, what I might
have, and how I could be.
If only I could find the guts to take one
step away from fear and be me.
But each time I ease my foot in that
direction of happiness,
Fear whispers in my ear, causing me to
turn back in loneliness.
Fear, I'm afraid, is the only friend I got.

Today I realized that my comfortable
misery was killing me from the inside
out.
I had to go. I had to move. Comfort
without happiness is unsatisfying
I took a step toward courage today, and it
grabbed my arm, and we ran away.
Never looking back for the fear left, I
followed courage.
Along the road, we found hope, which
pointed out happiness, and happiness
showed me, love.
All this I have found from one single step.
A step I took with courage.

-   Luna Charles

Chapter X

Where the earth ends, and the water meets the sky, you will find peace...

I walked across the hall to Jim and Bear's place and knocked long and hard against the hollow wooden grey door. For a minute, the noise I was making drowned out Mike's. Then, finally, the bear answered the door while in mid-yawn.

"Hey, what's up? You, okay?" he said while looking down at me.

His dark hair looked like it hadn't seen a comb in at least two days, his breath smelled like day-old beer, and the bags under his green eyes told the story of the late-night drug fest.

"Look, I'm sorry. I didn't mean to wake you up. It's just that Mike and I got into it, and I locked him outside on the patio. I don't want to talk to him right now, but I don't want him stuck out there," I said while fidgeting with one of my braids. My arms felt warm as if my body temperature was boiling from my pent-up anger.

"Sure, no problem, I'll let him in. Are you okay?"

I didn't answer his question, preferring to leave my problem to myself.

"Good. Wait until I'm at least at the bottom of the stairs before you go over there. Thanks, babe." I kissed him on the cheek and took off. I flew down the three flights of stairs, two steps at a time, while my purse repeatedly slammed into my hip, almost forgetting about my previous fall earlier.

Iran to my car while pushing the black key to unlock the door. Yanking it open, I slid in behind the wheel. I knew, without a doubt, Michael would come after me. He hated not getting a chance to convince people of his take on things, and this situation, too, I'm sure, was no different. Taking a second to adjust my seatbelt, I saw Michael coming after me down the stairs in the rearview mirror just as I was closing the door and engaging the lock. I started the Mirage and put it in reverse, nearly running him over as the car sped backward from the parking space. He jumped out of the way and ran to the side of the vehicle in time to grab the door handle, but I changed gears and sped off just as he was about to pull open the rear driver's side door.

Tears running down my face and blurring my vision, I bent down for a split second to pop Seal's CD into the radio. The horn from an oncoming car made me pop back up from looking at the black CD holder in fright. The redneck's eyes with the poorly kept goatee were almost as wide as his mouth, screaming all kinds of curses at me. I took a sharp right turn out of the way, tires squealing from the sudden movement, nearly missing the green Jeep from the opposite direction. The guy kept cursing at me even while I drove away, leaving Michael standing in the parking lot.

My heart beat against my chest like a sledgehammer. I didn't know where I was going, and I didn't care. Sarasota was his city, after all. Everyone I knew was his friend. I wanted to drive home, run into my mother's house, throw myself into her arms, and cry. However, that I knew was as likely to happen as God coming down and solving all my problems just by praying. My mom and I simply did not have that type of relationship.

The expression "I love you" was not spoken in her household. If you didn't realize she loved you by how she worked hard, protected, clothed, and fed you, then you were bound to have an emotional assurance problem. In fact, I've had a lot of, ever since that day when I had been ballsy enough to ask why she never said I love you to me. To my mother, the talk was cheap. If you loved her, prove it; you were wasting her time if you could not do it to her satisfaction.

Early in life, I realized that all I did for my mother was a waste of her time. She reminded me of that every time she called me a 'good for nothing whore, that would never amount to anything.'

What can I say? She was a strong woman with a disturbing way of disciplining her children. You may disagree with her methods. Maybe, if I were a different person, I would have cracked under pressure. However, I believe my desperate want to prove her wrong got me through everything I encountered.

I drove out of Beneva Place and unto Beneva Road, heading north toward Clark Road. Again, I pushed the CD track select button forward until the fourth track came on. Then, seal's soulful voice again filled my ears and the car.

"Don't be so hard on yourself ..." I cried harder. This was the first CD I had ever bought, and every time my mother went off on me, I used to put it on. But, somehow, his words always reassured me that I was not the only person with these problems.

Making a left on Clark, I headed west. The traffic was light. Everybody was at work. When "Fast Changes" ended, I realized where my subconscious guided me.

I pulled over into a Mobil station and parked out front. Pulling down the visor, I looked at myself. I couldn't walk in there looking like I did. Opening my purse, I fished out the face powder and gloss and fixed my face to appear more normal before entering the convenience store. As I walked in, a guy pumping gas into a black Lexus stared at me as if he wanted to say something. I didn't pause, just continued into the store. I returned to the beverage refrigerator and grabbed a four-pack of Miller Highlife, the cheapest beer.

The word 'pregnant' went through my head, but I dismissed it as fast as it came and grabbed the pack anyway. I walked up to the cashier. He was a twenty-something dark-haired guy with a shark tooth around his neck. He stared at my voluptuous chest like he wanted to be breastfed. I sat the pack of beer on the counter with a loud thud!

"Hey, can I join the party?" he said while using the laser scanner to get a price for the beer.

Usually, I would have been more personable, maybe even flirting with him. But not today. I was in no mood.

"No thanks," I said, not even with a smile, as I returned the beer he had placed inside the brown paper bag to the car.

I downed most of one of the sixteen-ounce cans as soon as I was behind the steering wheel. And in the privacy of my car. I continued toward my preordained destination while repeatedly looking back in the mirror for cops. Being arrested for a DUI is not something I can afford right now, but my mental state craved a beer.

I reached the beach just as "Newborn Friend" came on. Parking was tricky, even on a Thursday morning when I figured most people were at work or school and traffic had been so light. Finally, after about fifteen minutes, I squeezed the little Mitsubishi between two convertibles.

"I'm Alive" came on. I sat there listening.

"I fell on my feet this morning. Two angels heard me cry. This is your fate hereafter, take hold and be its master."

I sat there on the grey cloth seat of the little white Mitsubishi, letting the light penetrating through the windshield warm my arms and face. Inhaling the words, I tried to use them to fortify my spirit. I had gone into this relationship only a month after Daniel and I broke up.

Trying desperately to prove to myself that I was not the fuck-up my mother always said I was because it seemed every relationship I was in was doomed from the start. I wanted desperately to show Daniel that I didn't need him and could move on without him. Only now to face that I only proved my mother right and showed Daniel that I could not do better than him.

I will not let this break me. I will not tolerate this break me. I will not let this break me. So, as I lingered in the little car under the hot sun, I kept repeating those six words like a mantra.

The song ended, and I did not feel any better, but at least I had stopped crying. I reached down past the seat and popped open the trunk. I left the keys and the beer inside the front cabin. I went to the trunk to remove my beach chair and little leather cooler, always inside the car.

Moving the jack out of the way and an old T-shirt in there from the last time I was at the beach, I grabbed the cooler and saw it. It must have been buried under the shirt at the far end of the trunk. Jeanne gave me it a little over a year ago for my birthday. Michael and I had been two months into our relationship then. It had been so thoughtfully wrapped in red paper and a bow.

It meant the world to me when she gave it to me. It had been the only thing I had received on that birthday. Forgetting the other items, I picked it up and stared at the half-sun, half-moon mural decorating its front cover. *"Destiny" is* inscribed between the monarchs of day and night.

How could I have forgotten about this? I had spent so many nights pouring my pain into those tan-lined pages. It must have been in my trunk since I moved to Sarasota more than six months ago, and things were so hectic I hadn't missed it. Having always believed that things happen for a reason, I took the notebook with me even if I didn't always listen or pay attention. I went back into the car and loaded the beer into the cooler. I slung the cooler and black canvas that contained the chair over my shoulder, grabbed the keys and the journal, and headed west toward the beach.

The beaches and crowds here on the west coast of Florida are nothing like the east coast. Instead of rigid bodies, perfect plastic tits, and people from every country strolling along the sand, older white folk with canes and American snowbirds walked around. Not one foreigner, as far as the eye could see. And only a hand full of black people for that fact. It was as if Sarasota had somehow managed to segregate itself. I felt exposed in times like this position like I didn't belong. How I wished Michael was with me.

Nevertheless, I liked being here even without him and with the apparent racial divide. Especially since the beaches were so beautiful. As stunning as any virgin coastline that had yet to be stained by the human species. There was less development, less foreign tourism, and less havoc on the coastline. The sand was the same texture as granulated sugar, only finer. But best of all, ten minutes would get you to the beach no matter where you were.

My love for the sea was as ingrained in my hair color. Maybe it was that I was from an island, but whatever it was, I could never imagine living somewhere where I couldn't get to the ocean in less than an hour, even though I couldn't swim. The attraction to the water for me is its continuity. No matter what is happening, I can always rely on the beach to be there. It was the only place I thought was left on earth where I couldn't be mad for too long. So that afternoon, I walked through that sugary sand, heading west toward the sound of crashing waves. Setting my chair a few feet away from where the surf was rolling in, watching as each panel of water vanished into the sand just a few inches away.

I sat on that seashore and let the meditating effects of eons of endless waves wash over me.

The sun's rays reflected off the pearl-white sand blindingly. Removing the hair tie, which had held my hair in a bun, I let my braid fall down my back. A few strands caught in the wind flew about liberally. I took off my shirt, sat down in shorts and Victoria's Secret black lace bra, and dared the sun to burn me. Reaching into the cooler for a beer, I pulled out a can of Miller and took a deep swallow. The fizzing gassy drink ran down my throat and into my stomach, causing a lifted sensation.

I looked down at the bag I had placed near my leg and was about to reach for my phone when this perfectly tanned, dark-haired, chiseled kite flyer almost ran right over me.

He had looked up, navigating the course of his paper dragon in the sky by tugging at the cord in his hand. Then, when he looked at me for a split second too long, he tripped over the shoulder strap of my cooler and landed at my feet. The kite in the air yanked forward from his sudden loss of footing.

"I'm sorry." He stared at me. His eye apologized to my breasts before he saw my eyes. The dragon landed a few behind him, away from the surf.

"It's okay. I'm not hurt, no harm, no foul," I said while getting up to help him. As he stood, I realized how tall he was, a little over six feet, maybe six inches taller than me. He bent down and used both hands to dust off his Hawaiian floral print knee-length shorts. I noticed a school ring on his finger and which college he was from.

His eyes were the same color as the sea behind him, and I would have pegged him for another pretty Sarasota boy if it weren't for the dreads in his hair. But, instead, I smiled at this. He had an edge to him, I thought.

"Great, that's great. I mean, I wouldn't want to hurt you or anything." He bent down again to retrieve the cone holding the cord connected to his kite.

"My friends and I are hanging out over there." He pointed further down the beach in the same direction his kite had landed. I could see a series of kites in the air, though they were too far to make out any distinctive shapes. He took another quick look at my figure.

"Uh, well, do you maybe want to join us? My way of making up for getting sand all over you ..." He looked around, realizing he had not gotten any sand on me, only on my cooler. He figured he did not have a good enough excuse for asking me to join him, so he started backpedaling.

"... I mean ..."

"No, it's okay, really. I would rather be alone," I said, it being the truth.

"Well, I'm sure I could ditch them briefly and chill with you. I'm Eric."

I looked at Eric, tall, good-looking, with perfectly aligned teeth and pretty feet. He definitely didn't look like he had to work hard for anything. And the fact that he was sitting at the beach on a weekday without a care in the world told me he was probably here on vacation. He seemed happy. I wished I were that happy. I wondered . . . maybe if I hung out with Eric, just for a few hours, then perhaps that happiness would rub off on me.

"Look, thanks for the offer, but ...."

"I promise I'll behave." Eric held up his right hand in the boy scout oath.

I was tempted. What better way than to get back at Michael? First, to forget what was wrong with me, then to be around somebody I could not help but smile at each time, I looked at him, even if it was only for his looks. However, I knew this was not the answer.

"Thanks, but no thanks. Maybe next time I run into you." Finally, I decided to cut him short. He was cute, but cute white men with an edge had gotten me into enough trouble for now.

We stay there looking at each other for a second, his eyes pleading with me.

Finally giving up, he pulled a pen out of his pocket and asked me for a piece of paper. I fished the beer receipt from my purse and handed it to him. He wrote his number on it, told me to call him any time, and left in the direction of his fallen dragon and friends.

I watched him jog away, constantly looking backward at me, maybe hoping I would change my mind. Finally, he picked up his kite, turned around, and waved at me to come. I shook my head no. He blew me a kiss and went running toward his friends.

I hadn't been surprised by his reaction to me. I am a pretty woman. Skin is the color that I have realized both black and white people are envious of, not too dark or light. I speak correctly and carry myself as a woman, but I am not afraid to go into most hoods of situations. Maybe it was because I had turned myself into a chameleon as a kid, so people wouldn't pay too much attention to me.

I watched him until his shape faded into the distance.

I returned to my chair and noticed the journal at the foot of my seat. I don't remember it coming out of the bag when I gave Eric the paper, but I bent over to retrieve it. Then, sitting back down, I opened the journal with the red binder. Inside the front cover, Jeanne had inscribed:

To a dear friend,

Not much of a gift, but I hope you like it. Sometimes it's good to write what you feel when you feel it. Once in a while, when you're looking back. You can either regret the way you felt & take steps to prevent it from happening again ... Or you can smile at the art you created & relive priceless moments again & again.

As we grow older, memories will be the most precious thing we have!

Yet, while we are young, we can refresh ourselves continually to better shape our own destiny!

I love you, girl!

'...to better shape our own destiny.' I flipped through it; stopped at a page where I had written something last year when Michael and I had broken up for the first time.

My heart is as simple and delicate
as any flower.
Intricate in its pattern.
Deceptive in its power.
A beat as steady as any marcher's drum.
A rhythm as strong as one person's
conundrum.
Yet, for all its strength and stability.
My heart cannot take much duplicity.
Lust being called love is stupidity.
Entrapping me in the confusion of
identity.

Lost in what seems to be my own reality.
Begging God for answers to my own destiny.
Only to find myself living in purgatory.

Indeed, my words were so sad, so pained. A couple more pages, more grief, from the beginning of the book to where the writing ended. The journal was half-filled with nothing but hurt and despair written on sheets of paper. It was as if I had unwittingly spent my whole young adult life only concentrating on the negative. I was only twenty-four years old. Though I may not have had as many emotional problems as some people my age, it seemed like I had at least enough to fill half a book. Happiness had not entirely eluded me.

Though I may have encountered the worst in humanity, I have experienced some of the best. Why had I spent so much time focused on the sadness?

Why? That I didn't know. That was something that I would have to discover. I had free will. My decisions were ultimately mine. However, others may try to guide those choices for what they perceive to be the better.

As I sat there and thought about it, Jeanne was definitely right. Writing how you feel at a specific time allowed you to "regret how you felt and take steps to prevent it from happening again." I stared at the empty pages succeeding two years of emptiness and grief. Started at the waves on the beach on this momentous day, where so many endings and great beginnings existed.

I realized the time had come to see, be, and live. Not just to exist amongst others smiling while I quietly withered inside. I had pain, fear, and hurt in my hand. It was time for me to change it, to be alive instead of just living. So, I stared at the book and decided to write for another reason besides grief. I decided to do it for enlightenment, empowerment, and life.

I put pen to paper to acknowledge my past, accept my present, and plan for a better future full of hope, passion, and success.

I needed to find the Selene I had lost and learn why I had lost her.

Chapter XI

Time is on my side...

My mother died almost seven years before I was born. Isn't it ironic that such a troubled life should start with death on its heel? A rheumatic fever she caught while traveling in some Central American country murdered her. But, of course, my grandmother thought Voodoo had done her child in even after the prognosis. Fortunately, the good doctors of Centre Dequine Seven Day Adventist General Hospital were able to bring her back, voodoo or not.

However, only barely. My mother stayed in a coma for a year after that. The doctors were grim regarding her recovery, but my grandmother never gave up. Calling unto her all the herbal medicine she knew of, spirits far and wide, and favors she could never pay back.

When she did rise from the bed that so many had assumed would be the last resting place of her spirit, they presumed she would never walk nor be able to bear any children. Huh, what did they know? She was seventeen when she died and came back in stasis; she had me in January 1980 at twenty-four years old. In December of the same year, she had my sister. You do the math.

My family was always overprotective of us. My grandmother, a dark-skinned, strong-willed mountain woman, thought we would be her only sired grandchildren from my mother. But as the years progressed and I learned who my mother was, I realized there were worse things to fear than only having one sister.

In '88, when I came to this country that night, I met my two little brothers, Pierre and Michelle. As it turned out, my mother had been pregnant when she left for America. She had Pierre a few months after she arrived and Michelle a few years later. Plus, she was four months pregnant.

That night, I was terrified when I stepped out of the grey Oldsmobile sedan and looked for the first time at the house I would live in. It was huge compared to the two-bedroom apartment six lived in back in Haiti. It seemed so cold. The three-bedroom, two-bath house in what could have been considered a good neighborhood in those days had a tan exterior with baby blue trim, lush grass on either side of the paved driveway, and one coconut tree as the centerpiece of the front yard surrounded by Ocean Pacific irises.

I did not feel like I belonged in a place like that. I stood there looking up and down the street, wondering where everyone was. There had always been so many people outside talking to each other where I was from, always children playing. I looked at the house next door, and no one was out. In fact, no one except us was outside. I wanted to cry. I took the quietness and emptiness of the street as an omen of emptiness to come into my life. How right I had been ...

My mother ushered me past the tan wrought iron post that connected the porch floor to the roof, and over the front porch and into the white tiled front room where my two brothers waited for us, with my uncle behind them. My mouth dropped when I saw him there. I hadn't expected to see him after all. My grandmother had told us he was visiting family in the country when we had woken up to find him missing a week before I got on the plane. But instead, he waved to me, and I smiled back, showing all my teeth before my vision returned to my brothers.

The pair just remained there staring at me for a while. Neither of my siblings looked happy to see me, each asking her questions in English. I stayed in the open doorway, feeling like I was on display. Finally, my mother must have told them to hug me because Michelle walked up and looked like only a one-year-old could. Holding his hands in the universal toddler sign that said, "Pick me up," I was happy to oblige, having him close like a toy. However, Pierre only parked there watching while my mother tried to nudge him toward me. Finally, reluctantly, Pierre walked up to me and placed one arm around my waist in a small hug before he quickly let go and ran out of sight.

I stopped to look at the words that had flowed out of me. Like the currents of the great Egyptian Nile River. An odd place to start in my journey for answers to my troubling problems, but a start anyway. I let the flow continue unopposed. My pain was caused enough to allow the words to find their own end. *The house was a constant traffic of visiting people when I first came to this country. My mother loved to cook. Her beauty and mastery of the kitchen assured that whenever she cooked, people would show up to eat, drink, and converse. Having no one around my age to hang out with during those times, I ate, drank, and wrote.*

The latter two were my only salvation from eternal boredom and depression slowly growing inside me. My mother never had time for me, not like a mother should. I was more of an assistant and a babysitter to her than a daughter. However, when my stepfather started paying me attention, I was thrilled. I was happy to bring him food, drinks, or whatever he needed. I felt somewhat better about myself for almost three whole months having somebody pay attention to me.

Then one night in late March, he got sick. I wanted to play good daughter, so I made him soup and took it to him in bed while my mother was in the kitchen at the rear of the house trying to get my brother Michelle to eat. Then, as he often did, my stepfather asked me to join him on the bed while watching a war movie. So, I climbed on the king-size bed and sat beside him, my hands resting on my thighs. He looked at me and said that it was okay to relax. After all, he is my father, even if not by blood.

He said come lay your head on my chest so you can be more comfortable, which I did. Slowly he began to caress me, running his fingertips over my shoulder. The touch made me uneasy, but I stayed because I didn't want to upset him. Then his hand moved lower, over my small chest and down my legs, stopping at the edge of my skirt. He paused for a minute before moving up underneath the dress. Pushing his hand back, I jumped up and ran out of the bedroom, through the dining room, kitchen, and back door.

There I waited, scared that he would follow me, not knowing what to do or say, but after a while, I realized he wasn't coming. My uncle must have heard me slam the back door because he came looking for me. Through tears and fear, I told him what had happened. Silently, calmly, and coolly, he told me how I had deserved that treatment. How could I have been so nice to that man? Did I not understand what he had put my mother through for me to come here? He threw me a towel, then told me to wipe my face and clean the kitchen. I never told anyone. After that night, I did my hardest to give Daddy enough space so that no matter what happened, he would never have an opportunity like that again.

I threw myself into my schoolwork. My spoken English was bad. However, I excelled in math. Numbers are a universal language. Anywhere in the world you go, two plus two will always equal four. You just have to learn to pronounce the names of the numbers correctly. I won honors I did not clearly understand and was delighted by the attention I received from my teachers. I begged my mother to attend the award assemblies, but she was always too busy. Therefore, I always received my certificates the next day in class from my teacher, protected in the folds of a manila folder.

The summer that marked my transition from fourth to fifth grade was eventful. I had somewhat adjusted to my new environment, learning English and watching cartoons with the boys. My chores had become a routine that I no longer abhorred. Plus, my mother decided to divorce my stepfather after a fight they had one night.

She announced this to him as he woke in a pool of blood with a gun pointed at his head. My youngest sister, Jennifer, was born a healthy screaming one-month-old. As it turns out, he had cheated on her, not with one, but two women. One of them was his ex-wife. She had not wanted to end the marriage. A man cheating on a woman was not uncommon in our culture.

I mean, I think the belief among the women was not to give up somebody supporting you just because he couldn't keep it in his pants. However, that night he had decided to place his hands on her to physically harm her. Well, let's just say that was not a good idea on his part.

I had stood in the bedroom hallway watching as he had held her by the throat screaming at her. Tears ran *down my face as I held my brother's back and begged him to let my mother go. My mother kept telling us to go into our room through fits of coughs and broken words, but we couldn't move. We were too scared. I was about to let go of my brother, throw caution to the wind, and go after him.*

But just as I got the nerve to move, I saw my mother's hand reach a solid stone Native American statue behind her on the wall unit shelf he was pushing her against. The sound of cement hitting flesh echoed against the wall as she hit him over the head, breaking off a chunk of the Chief's feather-decorative headdress.

I wasn't sorry to see him go. In fact, it was quite a relief not to be scared to be alone with him in the house. What sucked was that my mother went from being too busy to not even being there, now working sixteen hours a day to pay all the bills. I went from having chores to being a mom. My uncle did his best to help, but with soccer practice and school, he hardly had any free time. Slowly, my mother didn't have time to cook or talk as time passed. Gradually, the house, once so alive with visitors, became empty of people, but the drinks were still there, and I still used them to appease my loneliness and boredom. My life consisted of school, family, and nothing else. Every time I would ask my mother if a person I had befriended at school could come over, her answer was simply,

"No. You don't need friends. Play with your brothers."

So, when she bought a somewhat used red bike, I guess as a gesture of appreciation that summer, I'm sure it was not with the intention of me making friends but of me being happier while playing with my siblings.

The first time I got on that bike in the front yard, I must have resembled an untrained monkey on a unicycle. My uncle and brothers watched me use the post for balance as I sat on the black rubber banana seat. Letting go of the post, I tilted straight and went around the coconut tree twice before falling. The *three almost fell to the floor laughing. Helping me get the bike off my leg, my uncle held it up for me to sit on, gripping it tightly with both hands until I was comfortable. Finally, he let go, and I took off down the block.*

I stopped writing for a minute, taking a moment to remember that eventful afternoon going around the block when I had met Gloria. I had made it halfway around the block before I felt lopsided on someone's lawn. I wasn't hurt physically, but my ego certainly took a bruising as a Latin girl, and a man I assumed was her father came running from across the street to see if I was okay. She couldn't have been much older than me, which made me feel worse because I was sure she knew how to ride a bike.

"You, okay?" he asked, moving the bike off me.

As her dad picked me up and I dusted myself off, I realized I knew the girl. She and I were briefly classmates before I was transferred out of that class because I was an immigrant. In the U.S.A., it seemed the education system had an unwritten rule to put everyone not physically born within the States a grade back, even if you were more intelligent than your peers.

My mother always said, "Friends are nothing but trouble." I wish I had paid more attention to this advice while writing this. She also said that men only want to use you until there's nothing left for them to use. This statement she was right about as well. However, I had willingly been involved in trouble with my friends. And I had allowed the men to use me every single step of the way. Now I realize I did not understand what I had hoped to accomplish from the allowance of such abuse. Gloria stared at me for a while until the memory clicked.

"I know you. You were in my class, weren't you?"

"Yes, I believe so," I answered while fidgeting with my hands.

"What is your name again?"

"Selene," I said, still fidgeting with myself and a little worried about the time I had been gone from home.

Her dad just stood there watching the exchange and holding my bike.

"Yeah, that's right, Selene, you had only been in my class for a week, then they took you out. Somebody said it was because you were not smart enough to be in," there," she said as she took my bike away from her dad.

"It's okay, Daddy, I know her. I'll help her home," she told her father.

Gloria's father smiled and kissed her forehead. Before returning to finish the yard work. I watched the whole exchange with a bit of jealousy. But, as I replaced my full attention to her, I realized she was speaking without me listening. Her dark hair was tied in a ponytail with two strands falling on opposite sides of her apple-shaped face.

"I don't know if you remember my name. It's Gloria," she said as she handed me the bike.

I didn't really look at her straight on as she was talking. I mean, I never looked at anybody straight on in those days. Too afraid of how people saw me, I guess. But Gloria wasn't really looking at me either. She was too busy talking and constantly gesturing as she spoke. First, Gloria pointed to her house across the street. It was identical to mine, except hers was white with blue trim. Then her gaze traveled slightly to the left, and she told me Laneika lived right there, pointing to a house caddy cornered to hers.

As she pointed, I looked at her pale outstretched arm in front of me and all the meat that surrounded her joints. I looked down at my darker, stick-like arms and realized how thin I was compared to her. In Haiti, the fatter you were, the wealthier you were seen as being since only the rich could eat plentifully. I wondered if she knew I had been poor just from looking at me.

I silently prayed that was not the case and carried myself as my mother had taught me. She told me plenty of times that no matter how much you have, if you take yourself with pride and confidence, people will think you have everything.

When I finally came own head, I realized whose house she had just shown me. I was amazed. I knew Laneika, too. She had been in my third-grade class, and we had almost fought. Laneika was very outspoken and confrontational, not afraid to say what she meant when she meant it.

To her, teachers who were unwilling to see her way had to become the subject of daily verbal assaults, even if they were said under her breath.

I had been in class with her for nearly six months but had never spoken to her since I was very concerned about how I sounded to other people since my English was not that good. So, she sat in front while I sat as far away from anyone as I could, hardly raising my hand to use the bathroom unless I thought I would pee on myself. Our teacher had been a petite, blond woman with hazel eyes that smelled like flowers.

I loved her because she had tried hard to make me feel comfortable and because she was a teacher. But unfortunately, being able to attend school in Haiti was reserved for the privileged few, and educators were treated like gold.

Anyway, one day, Laneika was very unhappy about her grade on a test and yelled at Ms. Fields disrespectfully in front of the class. Sitting in the back of the room, I could feel my anger growing at her bold disrespect toward our teacher. Finally, Ms. Fields told her to stand in the corner until it was time for a physical education class. That was not satisfying enough to .me. Later on, the coach came and got us, walking us in two straight lines to the field. After we had done our group exercises, instead of me going off by myself to walk the area as I usually did, I walked up to her and pushed her.

"What makes you think you are so special that you could talk to my teacher?" I shouted at her

"What are you crazy?" she asked. Why the hell is it your business how I speak to my teacher? She shouted back

Trying my hardest not to lose my infamous temper, I shove her again. More challenging this time, to the point that she fell down.

"Leave Ms. Fisher alone or else," I said in my bad English

She was about to get up and come after me when couch Burg saw us. Grabbing a hand full of my blue Physical education uniform shirt, he dragged me to the little cement hut on the side of the field, which he used as an office

"Geez, kid, you spend the whole year not talking or playing with anyone, and the first time I get any action out of you, you're fighting." He said while writing me a note

"Well, you'll have to go to the principal's office. But I don't think she will do anything bad to you since you have never gotten in trouble before." He continued

I said nothing, only remained there with my head down, scolding myself for getting in trouble.

"Well, here you go, Selene. Take that to Mrs. William."

I walked out of the office, note in hand, and, as slowly as possible, took what my first trip to the principal's office was, but certainly not my last. I laughed aloud as I remembered the look of shock on Laneika's face that day. I started writing again.

Therefore, I became friends with a Nicaraguan Princess named Gloria Diaz at twelve years old because of this incident. As she walked me back home, I was afraid of what my mother would say, but when we got there, she wasn't home, so I didn't tell her anything. However, the next day Gloria showed up unannounced at our front door, her bike at her side, wanting to know if I wanted her to teach me how to ride.

I answered the door, but within seconds, my mother was at my side, about to give an excuse about why I could not go. Advising Gloria to give me a minute, I begged my mother to let me go. We would only go around the block a couple of times. Just as I thought tears would come to my eyes, she surprisingly agreed, warning me not to go home after dark. I dashed out of the house without even saying thank you before she had a chance to change her mind.

I followed Gloria as best as possible, following her directions to relax and guide the bike with my body. Finally, she led me to Laneika's house, where she knocked on the door and asked her to come out and play. The dark skin, athletic-built girl stepped out of the red and white house wearing jean shorts and a lime green top. She gave me one look of annoyance as if to say what I was doing there. Unfazed, I stared back at her, knowing she did not scare me. Although our principal made me apologize to her, we hadn't talked since the incident.

She stood there for a while, looking at me, asking Gloria where I had come from. Gloria explained to her in a matter-of-fact way that I lived around the corner, and I was now her friend. I remember feeling the joy of hearing someone call me a friend for the first time. Laneika hadn't said anything to me as she got her bike, and we all rode. It would be two weeks before she would say anything to me, and by then, the past was the past, and we were all friends.

Gloria was one grade higher than me so that summer marked her move from elementary school to junior high. She had one sister who was just slightly younger than Pierre. Her parents were still together, and both worked. So needless, her responsibilities were relatively less than mine were. Laneika was in the same grade as me, though no longer in the same class. She also only had one sibling, a little brother Michelle's age.

Although she only lived with her mother. Laneika's father was always close at hand to provide her with anything she set her heart on. So blessed with the latest in everything, games, clothes, shoes, etc. I felt blessed as their friend for having the opportunity to just play with them and their things. Even if it was just a few hours a day after I had done all my chores.

In the beginning, Gloria and I hung out more with each other than with Laneika. At first, I thought it was because Gloria's mother was strict about whom she could have over; later, I learned otherwise. Gloria did not like Laneika very much, though I was unsure why. As I got to know Gloria better, I realized she was snobby toward anybody who did not do things the way she liked. I guess Laneika being Laneika, was not having any of that.

I was so desperate for a friend that I did not care what we did. When I went to her house, she would put makeup on me, do my hair, and play with me like a doll. I never thought anything of it. My most significant problem with her came one day when she said she could not find anything wrong with me except for the fact that I was Haitian. She went on to explain that being Haitian was not cool. They came over in boats and were poor, and everybody made fun of Haitian people.

I had sat there quietly for as long as I could. Listening to Gloria before all the blood that had started boiling in my veins became so loud that I could not hear anything else. I popped up from my sitting position on her bed and glared at her. I advised her that I was proud of being Haitian and that my culture was full of color, history, and strength. I never found reasons not to tell everyone where I was from. However, apparently, I was the only one of my peers with that belief.

I reminded her that even though to them, my country and its people were something to be ridiculed and persecuted, it had been the first Black Country to free itself from slavery, and yes, it had seen its share of bad times. From the day that it declared its independence to now, there has been one series of problems after another. I knew this. I had lived through two civil wars. However, that did not mean I was going to denounce my heritage.

After I was done and somewhat calmer, I looked at her and realized that my outburst had rather scared her. So, I apologized, and she, in turn, went back to what we were doing, though there was definitely tension from that moment on between us.

Elementary gave way to junior high, and we remained friends. Now and then, I would come against some idiot that did not like me and make a comment about my people, which I was quick to correct. Gloria, being the one in a higher grade, meant she had more friends and was more thoroughly versed in the affairs of teenagers than I. Therefore, she always tried to persuade me to be more accepting of the kids making fun of Haitians. I should try to fit in more and not make so many waves. I looked different from my people, so I could pass for being from another country.

"Why don't you just tell people you are from the Dominican Republic? It's close enough," she had said once. I hadn't even answered or bothered advising her why I would never do such a thing. Because the truth was, I didn't even know why. While all the other kids from Haiti pretended to be from different places so others could accept them, I had chosen to go against the grain. In addition, I did not understand what a Haitian person was supposed to look like, and I was not going to lie about myself just so people could like me.

Gloria disapproved of this thought, stating that fitting in was more important than causing waves. Beautiful as she was, at only an inch shorter than I was, with long dark hair and matching eyes, you would have thought she had more confidence in herself and did not need the approval of others. I should have walked away from our friendship then. Yet, I kept her as a friend because, on occasion, she was a great person though a little delusional about the world.

That is not to say I was more knowledgeable, but I felt I had more *experience dealing with obstacles. At this point in Gloria's life, her father's rule on boyfriends was the only block she faced. Neither of us was allowed to date. But that never stopped her from being more interested in boys than in schoolwork. Gloria always had an in-school boyfriend whom she held hands with and kissed. I knew what she was doing was wrong, but I kept my mouth shut because she was my friend, and that's what friends do: support each other's secrets.*

I stopped writing for a second to remember the many secrets she had asked me to keep. And how relieved I was when she finally went on to high school three years later when I was in eighth grade. Left mostly alone since Laneika and I didn't speak that much, and to contemplate the rigorous mental challenge that my teacher put me through. They were not as challenging as I would have liked them to be.

Bored from the lack of a demanding curriculum and the lack of drama from Gloria's life, I joined a program the school offered to students who wanted to work while still in school. It required us to be in school two hours earlier and keep our GPA in all classes at a high C. I almost laughed when I received the application and looked at the requirements. Nevertheless, I believed the program would give me the reward of having actual money to buy things for myself and not entirely relying on my mother, which was more valuable than any so-called real-life experience it advertised.

The first day of that program, I remember, felt like the first day of school. My stomach had been so full of butterflies that I had spent the night not sleeping but daydreaming about what might be. As I had entered the school that morning at seven to the silence and emptiness of the pre-hour classes, a slight fear of the unknown filled me with what might go wrong, but I pushed it aside and kept going.

Then, as I reached the cold metal doorknob, I paused to say a silent prayer to God that things would be okay. Not great, but hopefully better in my life with this step. I remember walking into an empty class. The only person there was a tall older gentleman with chocolate-brown skin and a balding head. He had sat lightly on the desk reading a manila folder, flipping through the pages with his right hand that contained a large gold pinky ring. His caramel belt matched his shoes, offset by the neatly pressed pair of khaki pants and short sleeve navy and cream polo shirt.

Looking toward the door, I had just walked through and then down to his gold wristwatch, he said that being earlier than everyone else was the trait of someone born to be successful, then he directed me to take a seat. Those words have stayed with me my whole life, as was the friendship I developed in that class.

I had remained there patiently in the empty class, reading a book, waiting for my fellow classmates to arrive while Mr. Sneil read his file. When the door opened, I looked up from the pages to see a petite Latin-looking girl walk in wearing a colorful green, red, and yellow short-sleeved shirt and shorts that reached her mid-calf. Mr. Sneil looked at his watch and told her that punctuality was required in the class and that two more tardiness would result in her dismissal. She shrugged and sat in front of me.

She turned around and tilted my book from my grasp so she could read the title while asking if it was a good read. I told her yes; I loved the author and had another book by him in my bag if she wanted to borrow it. She shook her head, yes and I went in my bag and gave her the book.

We spent the rest of the time talking before the class started. As it turned out, Jeanne had just come to the U.S. from Jamaica and was still adjusting. I told her I was from Haiti, had been here for years, and was still adjusting. As I mentioned where I was from, I was slightly anxious to hear her reaction. However, I exhaled a little when she continued with what she was saying without even a pause.

As Mr. Sneil began the class, she gave me a smile and turned in her seat by the end of the course. We walked down the hall together and talked like we had known each other for years.

And just like that, my friendship with Jeanne began, a Jamaican-Indian, take nothing from no-one girl, who stood a full head shorter than I but acted as if she was the toughest kid in school. However, Jeanne was not like any companion I had ever made previously. A few weeks into our friendship, she confided in me that she had Cystic Fibrosis, a hereditary lung disease that would kill her probably before she was thirty.

Jeanne said it so nonchalantly that I thought she was joking for a minute. Jeanne just was not. It is just how she was; Jeanne would not let the hand she had been dealt dictate who she was. Maybe that is why Jeanne was so uncaring about whether her actions were accepted by those around her. She did not care about my ethnic background, accent, clothes, shoes, or awkwardness. She was everyone's friend.

In addition, she found it absurd that anyone would feel the need to hide their identity. Her beautiful long, black curls, olive skin, confidence, and intellect made me instantly jealous of her. However, it was jealousy I could live with to be in her presence.

Resting here on the beach so many years later, I realized I spent a lot of time in my youth jealous of others for one reason or another without ever realizing that people were jealous of me, too. However, that year with Jeanne as a friend. My jealousy of others faded as I started enjoying the time spent with her by my side. I introduced her to Dean R. Koontz, who was my favorite writer. She, in turn, introduced me to "pot."

Jeanne and I spent most of our time when we were not cleaning and cooking for our own homes, writing, watching old Kung Fu movies, and by a mid-school year, working. That job would be one of the three things that happened that school year that would always be one of the defining moments in my young life.

The first was the job. It was in the school cafeteria, so now the kids did not just make fun of me for being Haitian but for now also for being a "cafeteria lady." The second was my friendship with someone I knew who accepted me for me and did not want me to pretend to be anything else. That friendship helped me out of my shell and put my guard down concerning what people might assume about me. And the third is what I believe should have been the most inconsequential, but apparently wasn't; Eric Schinocoff and I became friends, and he started walking me to class.

As insignificant as that act should have been, the fact that that particular boy started paying me attention sent my whole school into an uproar; well, at least it did among the students. Why? Five words, white, blond hair, blue eyes.

I think it wasn't the fact that Eric was white that bothered people so much. But the moment we started hanging out was when some of the Black guys stopped teasing me and started paying me attention in another way.

This drama gave me a feeling that I had never felt before, wanted. Boys were mad at other boys, and girls were jealous of me for the attention I was getting. It was a little elating. The interest made me more confident, I wasn't afraid to hold my head up, and with Jeanne by my side, I became more outgoing, though, in my head, I still wasn't by far popular.

My whole life was becoming more exciting just because of Eric. I didn't see that maybe Eric was paying me more attention because I was more confident about myself since I had a job that allowed me to buy things for myself, and I had a friend by my side that was not trying to change me. But, no, I didn't see that. I only saw this new excitement because of the white guy who liked me.

I reached down for the beer I had sipped, only to find the can empty once I brought it to my lips. Suddenly, I felt the heat of the sun upon me. I looked up from the pages of the diary for a second. And was almost blinded by the glare of the almost-white sand. Then, blinking my pupils back to a healthy size, I shed a tear. How long had I been out here? I wondered.

Closing the journal on my lap for the time being, I bent down to retrieve another can. The small black cooler was next to my bag, so I noticed a red light flashing from my phone as I entered the cooler. Forgetting about the drink temporarily, I picked up the cell. Five missed calls, four from Michael and one from Daniel.

Why would Daniel call me? I reflected. Daniel, the ex-fiancé, had almost had all of me and had lost it in one night. Daniel, who I was not sure I ever fully got over. Going from my relationship with him to the one with Michael so quickly, I never gave myself a chance to heal.

I took the journal off my lap with my free hand. Placing it on the sand next to my foot. While securing a new beer can between my knees, I pushed the send button on the phone keypad. I knew Danny would be at work, so I wasn't expecting him to answer. I just wanted to call and leave a message so he knew I had returned his call. I had not spoken to him in at least a couple of months. It was much more often than I thought I would when we first broke up.

"Hey, sweetheart." The sound of his voice sent tremors through me. Damn, I should have figured he would answer. "What's up, you at work?" he continued.

"No, I'm not at work," I said, not informing him I no longer had a job. My stomach started doing cartwheels as I spoke to him; I prayed my voice did not betray my physical reaction.

"How are you doing?"

"I think I should be asking you that. You don't sound like yourself, okay?" I could hear the concern in his voice. I couldn't tell him the truth because it would crush him. The pregnant part, not the breakup. I had a miscarriage while we were together once. It had been more upsetting for him than it had been for me. Until this day, he still wants to be with me, have a family, and live happily ever after. However, how do you forgive someone after they have cheated on you? How do you trust them again?

"I'm fine," I lied. "I'm just ... having a disagreement with Michael."

"About what? The fact that he's an asshole or doesn't deserve you ..." I heard him blow air out of his lungs.

"Why don't you leave him already?"

"Miami misses you, babe ...."

I could read between the lines. Miami didn't even know I was gone. He meant he missed me. But, moreover, a part of me missed him, too. Yes, he had cheated on me. However, I could not deal with that at that time.

"Danny, let's not go into this right now. Anyway, it was nothing big. I'm fine ... Look, I'll talk to you later, okay?"

I hoped he didn't hear the strain in my voice as I hurried to get off the phone with him, worried that I would suddenly break down and start crying, divulging all my troubles.

"Whatever you say, sweetheart. Call me later, all right? Remember, I'm here for you."

"All right, Danny. Bye."

"Bye."

I flipped the phone off and took a deep swallow of beer. I had been ready to spend the rest of my life with that man. I had really believed that Danny and I were in love at a point. I had forgotten everything I had learned about relationships from my mother and friends and started thinking he was different. We had been so good for so long; why had things gone so wrong between us so fast?

Indeed, we had fights, but who did not? That still did not explain what went wrong. The more I thought about it, the more it made me feel like Mike and I were going through the same thing. What was missing in all the relationships that made them eventually come to this? Was it them or me? My mind was churning with deductive thoughts, but nothing made sense. Every notion was muddled and incomprehensible.

Unable to decipher what possible problems could be causing such disastrous endings in my affairs, I cleared my mind and dialed home. But unfortunately, the wind raised its voice the same instant I pushed send. Now I wondered whether I imagined the wind's voice backing me up every time I did something related to Mike.

I paused briefly, reminding myself that I was not dialing home. It was not my home anymore, but his, 'Michael's. When the phone first rang, my breath was caught in my throat. During that second, I exhaled and was breathing somewhat normally. By the third ring, I was wondering whether he was even home.

"Hello."

This was the first time I heard him sound like he didn't know what he would say to me, and I didn't know what I wanted to tell him.

"Yeah, you called me." I tried to sound as nonchalant as possible.

"Baby girl, you know we need to talk about this. When are you going to come back home?" He was trying to sound caring, but he sucked at it.

"I'm at the beach. Talk, I'm listening."

"Selene, come home. I'm worried about you, and you shouldn't be alone, do not act like this!"

"Fuck you, Mike! I'll act however I feel!" I flipped off the phone.

In less than ten seconds, the cell rang. I stared at it in my hand. Michael's picture was flashing on the Samsung screen. I wanted to toss it in the ocean and have the salt water corrode the circuitry as time had our relationship. But, instead, I flipped it open.

"What?" I said, wanting to sound pissed off. But instead, my voice cracked like the break of a lightning bolt revealing the pain hidden under the surface

"I'm sorry," he said, the phony sincerity in his voice again. "Please come home. Let's talk."

"Yeah, well, don't. Don't be sorry for me."

"... That is not what I. meant."

"I will do all the worrying about myself from now on, thank you." I had started playing with that one rogue braid again

"Please come home."

I wanted to scream, cry, and pierce my skin with something sharp enough to cause excruciating pain to my flesh so that I knew for sure this was life and not a nightmare. However, none of that happened. I just agreed to go home, flipped the phone off, and dropped it into the bag, taking another deep swallow of beer. I retrieved the journal and kept writing.

Chapter XII

Times flies...

    Eighth grade flew by that year. Maybe it was because of all the drama or the fun I was having with the attention I was getting. Either way, I loved life by the time my fifteenth birthday rolled around. I decided to attend a Charter school for senior high without my mother's knowledge. She was still too busy to be bothered by what was going on with my life. I signed all things that required a parental signature.

    I thought going to a more elite school would give me better opportunities. Maybe I would become a doctor and be able to help my mother with the bills so she would not work so hard. Yes, we didn't get along, but that doesn't mean I didn't see the stress she was going through.

Plus, my "home" school didn't have the best reputation. I had heard that it was nothing but gangs and drug dealers. So, the day I decided, I walked out of the guidance counselor's office with two applications, knowing that Jeanne and going over there would be the best thing for us. When I saw her in the hall, I was so happy I blurted out the plans I had made for us without giving her a chance to speak.

She looked me sincerely in the eyes and told me that she didn't feel the same way. The school was only two blocks from her house and more manageable to get to than bussing to another school tens of miles away. I was crushed. Our friendship had become everything to me. With her by my side, I had begun to feel capable of anything.

That afternoon, she pulled me aside after school and handed me the application I had given her to fill out with all my information. She told me that I was her best friend and, as such, I deserved the best and not to let anybody, not even her, get in the way of that. The next day she walked me to the guidance counselor's office to hand in the application.

As I walked home from school that day, I was so full of love for having somebody like her as part of my life since my home life hadn't changed much. Except for Lenard and Lee, they were the nephews of the new neighbor that just moved in. They were both older than I was. Lenard, by three years, and Lee, by two. But nevertheless, they were cool.

They acted like my big brothers, the ones I always wanted. They introduced me to comic books, martial arts, baseball, and how to throw the perfect right hook. They made my home life livable.

A week before the last day of school, I got the acceptance letter to the new school and told my mom. She was happy, to my surprise. And even more so, I had taken the initiative to do what was best for me in her absence. Another surprise. When I told Jeanne, she hugged me and told me she would go to Jamaica for the summer but promised to bring me something really cool back. I told her she didn't have to; I would miss her a lot, but freshmen needed to attend summer class at the "Tech," which was the nickname of the Charter school I would be attending.

So, I would be swamped trying to keep up in high school because I had heard it would be hard, and hard work was something I was used to and prepared to do. Little did I know that the work was not the hard part of being in high school. The hard part was keeping out of trouble and away from drama.

When the last day of junior high came, people cried and gave hugs, but not me. The only two people I cared about I knew I would see again. Laneika lived around the corner though we didn't talk much then, and Jeanne would be back after summer. So, as I walked home that Tuesday afternoon, I floated on a cloud of pure anticipation for the future.

A week later, a postcard came in the mail telling me where my bus stopped and when the bus would pick me up. I looked long and hard at the 6:45 A.M. written on the small three-by-five card. It was an hour earlier than I would have needed to get up if I had gone to my home school. Finally, I resigned myself that it was for the best and returned to my chores.

I was terrified the first day I had to walk to the bus stop alone. My house was two blocks over, and the streets were empty and dark except for the street lights. I could hear dogs barking from everywhere, and I was sure that at any moment, a whole pack of them would spring up out of nowhere and attack me.

So, I took each step as quietly as possible, not wanting to inadvertently give away my position while praying with every step. When I finally got there, standing under a single street lamp were Gloria and Laneika.

The relief that washed over me was only surpassed by my happiness to see them and the surprise that Gloria was there. I ran to them and almost knocked

Laneika over when I hugged her. With Laneika, I wasn't surprised to see her there. I knew she was attending that school because everybody wanted to participate in the charter school then. However, why was Gloria attending summer school? After all, she would be a sophomore the next school year, so she didn't have to go.

I hadn't seen or talked to her in a couple of months, so I was stunned to find out she had failed English and had to attend summer school. When we first saw each other that day, we were so happy. God! I was so young then. Where did all the laughter go?

That summer, Laneika, Gloria, and I would wake up at 5:30 A.M. every morning to be at the bus stop at 6:45, though Gloria got up an hour earlier to do her make-up. This routine went on for a few months without incident. Until one morning ...

We all climbed the three steps onto the bus, one after another, like a row of ducks. Gloria was talking to me about some guy her friend Lula was hooking her up with. He was going to meet us after school. Suddenly, my blood turned cold. I hadn't been paying attention because I was in the middle of the most incredible scene in a book I was reading. Until I heard the word "us," I was not in the mood to relive the catastrophe that happened the last time one of her friends tried to hook her up. Therefore, I put my newest Koontz book aside as I slid into the window seat of the bus.

As we sat, I turned to her, keeping my place in the book with my middle finger. Then, looking directly at her, I tried to jog her memory of the prior occasion when one of her friends tried to play matchmaker. The guy had been so ugly she had locked herself in the girls' bathroom of our junior high school until he left.

Gloria remembered, but that didn't deter her from the planned meeting with this new guy. Besides, her girl Lula had sent her a picture, and the guy was supposedly hot. I shook my head in exasperation and kept reading. Then I thought of something, and it turned out I had nothing to worry about. She had already figured out how she would see this guy even though he didn't go to school with us and she was not allowed to date.

The plan was simple but well thought out. The guy's name was Ken. Ken would be meeting us at the bus stop after school. Then, he would walk us home so they could talk. And since Laneika and I would be with her if her father or mother happened to drive by our bus stop, she could tell them he was one of our friends, and I knew that was safe because our parents didn't really talk to each other, so nobody would ever have to lie to their parents except maybe her. So, I had to admit it would work.

That afternoon after the bus dropped us off. We had to wait ten minutes for Gloria's latest beau to appear. Finally, fed up with waiting, Laneika left, leaving me to wonder why I had agreed to the plan in the first place. I did not get the big deal when he finally showed up, long braids bouncing in the air as he jogged up to us wearing his dark blue jeans and an undershirt. I just turned around and started walking, and they followed suit. We walked home so slowly I thought I saw the neighbor's grass growing.

This scenario went on for weeks, then one day, Gloria came to us with the outline for another plan that she and Ken had come up with so that they could see each other more often. I was surprised then, but now I know I should have expected something from her. After all, she was always plotting for as long as I had known her.

Ken was a jock. He worked out six times a week and taught in a karate class part-time. The arrangement, again, was uncomplicated but, as always, well thought out. That afternoon Gloria and I would be conveniently hanging-out outside her house. Ken would come jogging by, recognize Gloria as an old friend from junior high, and stop to talk to her since he had just moved into the neighborhood. I had to admit the girl was good. The plan went off without a hitch. So, every day Ken came by and hung out with us outside. Eventually, I got tired of being the third wheel, so to speak. They didn't need me anymore, so I stopped going there just to be part of the ruse.

Preferring to spend my afternoons with my brothers, or Lee and Lenard, playing ball, reading comic books, and watching Anime, besides cooking, cleaning, and doing homework. Then one day, walking home from school, Gloria asked me a peculiar question. I remember this because this was the beginning of the end of my using good judgment.

She wanted to know why the only guys I had as friends were Lee and Lenard. She was worried about me. Apparently, people were talking about my only male friends being white. She and Ken thought it would be a good idea if maybe I met his friend. My answer was a simple—no. I didn't want to be hooked up with anybody and didn't care about people "talking." I had watched her and Laneika do the love thing, and they only ended up hurt. I had enough in my life to worry about. I didn't need a guy.

Besides, what was wrong with hanging out with Lee and Len. Oh, right, they were white, again, the white thing. Damn, and here I thought we had integrated as a people. Finally, we reached the corner by her house, so I stopped walking so we could finish our conversation. 'Just meet him,' she said. I told her no and walked away.

Over the next few days, Gloria made it her mission to talk me into the "meeting her boyfriend's friend" thing. It would be great, was her argument. She had ignored the "you only hang out with white guys" thing. By the fifth day, I gave up. It happened like this: We were in front of her house. She was talking to Ken about something.

By now, he was walking her home from the bus stop. And they were not hiding their involvement from her family. I was immersed in "The Bad Place," which I have to recommend to anyone who is a -mystery-horror reader.

Anyway, needless to say, I wasn't paying any attention to them. Just inputting the mandatory affirmation when I thought it was needed. I didn't realize that they had caught on to my act. Gloria snatched my book, ran into her house, and locked the wrought iron door. A trade, she proposed my book for my cooperation in the meeting. Damn! How could I refuse? I was at a delicious part. I agreed. So, this is how I came to be introduced to Mister Sean.

Wait, I have to change something. Meeting Sean was the beginning of everything going wrong. Gloria arranged the meeting, but I gave her my guidelines. It would be in front of my house, and Lenard would be a "backup." The day I met; Sean was the stupidest, most childish event in my history. It turned out that Sean didn't trust Ken's taste in women. So, he sent a scout ahead pretending to be him. The problem is, the *guy he sent, I knew. We had been in junior high together. He had even dated Laneika.*

If a dark guy could blush, David, Sean's friend, would have from embarrassment. He knew their plan was worthless when he recognized who I was. I was laughing so hard I hadn't noticed how truly pissed Len was over the "insult" of his "little sister." Len's usually sky-blue eyes were turning dark sea blue. And David, well, David wasn't dumb; he had moved to the other side of Len's uncle's car. I moved quickly between the two.

After all, Len was two hundred pounds, a high school senior, and lifted weights for fun. David, however, must have weighed ten pounds more than me and was four inches taller than Len, but no match whatsoever. David spoke so fast that his words ran together as he tried to talk his way out of becoming dog food. The whole scene seemed like an episode of Family Matters as I stood there when suddenly, from the corner of my eyes, I saw this person walking down the block toward us.

I had been through many things in my young life before I came to the U.S., weeks of hunger, not having a place to sleep, and walking miles with my grandmother and little sister to sell whatever people would buy to eat. I have witnessed a life that no child should ever have to store in their memory bank. People were burned in truck tires because of the civil war, machetes cut people open, and children begged for food. I felt a lot of different emotions in my life.

Most things I've blocked, others I've kept with me to remind me how strong I am. But, that night, hanging out in the back of Len's uncle's Cougar, I felt something I'd never experienced. I felt a desire for something I craved but yet could not explain. The tightening of the throat, the shortness of breath, and the fire burning from the inside out. I felt want, a sexual desire for the unknown stranger walking down the street. It was the first of such feelings for anyone in my life. Why? I didn't know.

I knew I had to know who this guy was for no recognizable reason. I had turned completely around to watch the approaching stranger without realizing what I was doing. The white cotton shirt he wore reflected against his dark skin and blue jeans while clinging to every well-developed muscle in his upper body.

He had a gentle swagger to his walk that screamed out his confidence without him uttering a word. He wore a dark blue baseball cap pulled low over his dark caramel face. Hand tucked into the front pocket of his jeans, but his lips, those large, soft, inviting lips. My whole world faded as I watched him walk toward me until nothing was left but the two of us.

Chapter XIII

Mind over matter...

A seagull flew overhead, squawking loudly to neither itself nor me, a weightless figure gliding underneath the cloudless sky. I looked to discover the sun had reached its zenith in the sky. Looking down at my wristwatch only to find that it was already 2:25 P.M. Damn, I had been writing for at least two hours. The tan lines on my body had already established themselves around the exterior of the bra top, and now if I did not move, even with the sunblock, I could be facing terrible sunburn. A feat I learned the hard way that even black people could accomplish.

Taking a glimpse at the ocean, I resolved to go home to face Michael and discuss the fate of my pregnancy. A conversation whose outcome I knew would not make the decision any easier.

"I didn't have a home," I mumbled aloud to hear the words reverberate into my ears, hoping that the sound of them going in, rather than being repeated over and over inside my head, would be different. It wasn't.

Closing the journal on my lap, I reached down for the beer. Saw the light flashing red on my phone again. Ignored it. I didn't have to pick it up. I knew who it was. It had been at least forty minutes since Michael had expected me to be on my way. Taking a bit too warm to be satisfying, swallowing from the gold aluminum can I had in my hand.

I emptied the rest in the sand. Then, looking around, realizing that still, the day's beauty had not morphed into anything that could be considered an ally for my demoralizing mood. Blue, crisp, perfect, I wanted to cry but somehow found the strength to keep it in. Tightening my throat made it almost impossible to catch my breath as I stood there for a minute fighting hyperventilation, contemplating my future. The wind blew from the west, caressing my face. Yet, somehow, I knew I was going to be okay. I did not know how I knew, but I knew.

I had read somewhere that all conscious beings could control their destiny through thought. It didn't have to be active. Most often, what affected our lives the most was inactive thought. The ideas that swam around in our mind when we were so focused on something that all we could think about was that one thing. That thought of how little money we had, how bad our relationship was, how ugly we felt, or how chubby we appeared to be.

The article said that when all you did was concentrate on the negative, all you would receive was negative. If we kept saying how little money we had, we would continue having very little money and so on with every other thought. Thus, the same was true for the opposite.

If this was true, I pondered, then my present circumstances must be the result of me beating myself up about how I was not good enough to be loved like I thought I should be. In addition, my train of thought was constantly thinking about how all my boyfriends had been jerks, and I deserved nothing but creeps because I was weak and needy. If that was true, then this was my fault.

Making up my mind to make the journey I had procrastinated against for so long, I ran my fingers through my hair, removing the rubber band that bound the braids together on my head. The strands fell, cascading over my shoulders in golden-brown tendrils. Like an Amazonian sorceress, the light caressed me, setting each braid on fire.

I saw my beauty as others saw it. I saw the men who were staring at me from a distance. I paid all of them minimal attention, too lost in my thoughts, fears, and my heart's desperate plea that this was not happening again.

However, it was, and maybe it was because I had concentrated so hard on keeping it from happening again. Perhaps I should not have thought about it at all. Instead, I should have considered how beautiful I was, how strong I was, and how the man I had in my life was the best. Maybe if I had, it would be true now.

Chapter XIV

The more things change...

It took me another twenty minutes to get back to the car through the hot sand, bright sky, and rigid bodies. I put the beach chair in the trunk, the beach bag in the back seat, and the cooler in the passenger seat since there was a beer left. I got in and drove out of the parking lot. The star, which the earth orbits, was ablaze in the clear blue Florida sky. With no sunglasses to protect my eyes, I squinted as I drove eastward from a westward-facing beach.

As I went, I tried not to think of what I had to face in my immediate future while I opened my last beer. Left on Stickney Point, which turned into Clark Road, making a right onto Beneva was as uneventful as any Thursday could be in a redneck town out shadowed by its big sister Miami.

I pulled into the parking space directly in front of the building, only available since all sensible people were at their nine-to-five. Lingering for a minute in the car, I looked up at the menacing figure in the dark, beige and white, three-story building cast directly in front of me. There in the sanctuary of the Mitsubishi Mirage, I finished the cheap domestic brew, mentally saying the "Our Father" prayer before having the courage to get out of the vehicle.

The day's beauty hurt me every time I stopped and took notice. It was the kind of beauty I thought Monet would have used, the sunlight shining down from the heavens to paint one of his famous water lily paintings. Cloudless with blue skies, I would have bet I could see God if I knew what angle to look up at. Bad things should not happen on days like this.

Carrying the beach bag in one hand and the cooler in the other, I made my way up the stairs, a bit light-headed from the alcohol and the drenching of UV in my system. By the time I reached the front door, I was out of breath and spinning. I stood there for a minute, juggling the bags to find the door key. When the door flew open, I had just placed the correct key in the doorknob. I jumped in surprise, almost dropping my bags.

Michael must have heard me or had been anxiously sitting on the edge of the couch, eating his fingernails while waiting for me to come home. Knowing him, he wanted to be as polite and sociable as possible until we resolved this problem.

He stood in the doorway, almost blocking my path. His face was composed, eyes smiling. He looked like he didn't have a care in the world. Yet, the mere sight of him irked me. It was a mixture of anger and agitation. Was it because I loved him that I felt this way, or did I feel like this because I couldn't believe I was ever with him?

"Hi, um, let me help you with that." He stepped forward and reached down for my beach bag.

"No, it's okay. I got it, thanks," I said.

As I squeezed past him and left the door open behind me. He pulled it shut. The air that flowed out of the apartment was forced to stop. Sending all the white vertical blinds into a slide. I put the bag down underneath the cream color particle wood kitchen counter's overhang. He brushed past me as he went to sit on the sofa, hesitating a second too long. I paused to let him by.

An electric current flew between our two bodies. I closed my eyes and allowed it to pass before I went to the kitchen. The room wasn't that big, barely eight-feet by ten inches, just big enough for the appliances, a sink, cabinets, a pantry, and two people to stand in without stepping on each other. I took the last Corona out of the fridge, popped off the top, and walked back into the living room. MTV's "Inferno" was on, but the volume on the TV was muted. A red team member was pummeling a purple team member with a spinning log. The rest of the members of both teams shouted, screamed, and yelled, all in silence.

I sat in the Lazy Boy cross-legged as if I was getting ready to meditate with a beer in my hand. I said nothing, just stared at the muted television, sipping my beer. The tension in the room was as thick as the hot chocolate my grandmother used to make me from pure cocoa beans when I was younger. I never really liked the auburn drink; it was too potent. Abruptly my chair went into a spin, coming to a stop in front of Michael on bended knees, tears dripping down his toasted beige complexion.

Sitting motionless, staring at him, he at me. I clinched the beer in my hand as if I could infuse my marrow with the glass from pure force and will that, in so doing, I could strengthen my resolve. That did not happen. Maybe it was for the best. After all, the glass was not strong and could break easily if the proper force was applied. I needed to be stronger than that.

A door slammed shut in an apartment below us. Neither of us flinched. We continued in our silent, motionless mental dance of dejection. I had started to cry, though I didn't even realize it until I heard the first soft *click* from the salty traveler that had made its way down my face to end its journey on the top of the Corona bottle.

With all the tenderness I learned was his to give and take as he saw fit, Michael removed the bottle from my hand. I looked away and closed my hands into little fists on my lap, so tight that my nails threatened to pierce the skin and draw blood.

He pried them open and held each entangled with his. The pressure with which I had violated my flesh had not ended because of his hands' insertion into mine. But instead, I sought to go through his hands to reach my own and continue with the self-mutilation. He neither flinched nor showed any discomfort but continued crying silently. Michelangelo's cherubs had a face like this, I thought. And I'm sure Lucifer was as beautiful when inviting you to sell your soul.

Slowly, he rose to his feet. My hands slowly released the claw-like grip I had on his. He bent down for a moment, covering me with his person; I felt the warmth and strength of his arms as one arm glided underneath my folded legs and one wrapped around my waist.

I gave him no assistance in what I knew he intended to do. Instead, he lifted me without effort. Not a grunt or breath escaped him. And like so many nights when he stole me away to bed for one purpose or another, he carried me now like any good prince to his bedroom chamber, not for love, but for a dialogue on mutual ground.

Michael and I had two rules. Both involved the bedroom. Neither had ever been broken by either one of us. The first and most significant was that neither of us could go to bed if the other was upset by something. The second, and what he intended on using now, is that if we were in the middle of a discussion and no end could be seen, we would lay in bed in each other's arms, just speaking, not caring if we made sense. Just lay there until we got it all out and hopefully made a mutual decision.

Therefore, in keeping faith in a rule that no longer mattered between us since our relationship had discontinued existing in one form or another, Michael carried me through the bedroom door and onto the bed with no injury. Clothing lay throughout the room. The lighting was mute because the only luminosity entering it came from what had managed to struggle through the closed vertical blinds. His cologne filled my nostrils. Unfortunately, the bed had not been fixed, so I was half on when he laid me down and half on the reversible plaid comforter.

I reached for a pillow near my foot, thought better of it, and wiggled across the bed to retrieve my stuffed bear. I must have looked like a pissed-off teenager refusing to speak to a parent or something. Mike must have guessed what I wanted from the general direction of my struggle. He walked around the bed, rescuing my ally in loneliness, and placed the stuffed animal in front of me. I gripped it, holding it within my arms in a way resembling the creature it was.

Absently playing with its red bow tie, I continued the silent purging of water through my eyes. Michael lay across from us, facing the bear and me. His face was now dry, empty twin riverbeds still visible on his face from where earlier the water had flowed. He raised his hand to my face to wipe away my tears. I twitched involuntarily from the anticipation of his touch. He moved his hand away, instead laying it over the arm holding Remy. His communication was as warm and gentle as I had awakened this morning.

"I love you, Selle. I'm sorry. I'll support you whatever you want to do," he whispered. He was so close I could feel his breath above my brow. I remained silent

"Selle, please say something ...."

"You didn't even ask ..." I started, then stopped.

"I know I was out of line. I was scared; I would never ask you to do anything you didn't want to do. I love you, you know that, right?"

I said nothing. Michael's hand closed around my arm. He moved closer, and now our knees were touching. Remy stuck between us, though unable to come to my rescue like the Marvel superhero he was named after; he was still saving me by not letting the enemy get too close.

"Selle, I would never ask you to do anything you were not ready for; you don't have to do anything you don't want to. You know that, right?"

Deep inside my head, as those words rolled off his tongue, a part of me considered the probability of getting away with murder. The other and probably the more rational part thought what he had just said was the most extensive line of bullshit I'd ever heard. And what's worse is that all men use that same fucking line to get what they want: sex, money, whatever. And we, as women, allowed it to work every time.

It always starts the same way, with the exact damn four words. In the same acclamation that provided us with an escape from the mistakes we were on the road to make. And the truth was, that escape was ours to take. We didn't have to do what we were on the verge of doing. We had the option not to take that so obviously 'easy to reach, but hard to get off' road of momentary relief. We really did not, but we do. We take it with eyes wide open, although maybe our minds are not too clear of thought.

Why? Is it because we believe in our hearts that it is as empty of substance as the Sahara is of water? This belief is that we can make everything as it used to be. When it was perfect and the afternoon light shone with a new brightness every day, and the bluebirds only sang the song he may have dedicated to you the night before. Then, when you were truly and undeniably, in love, if we only did this one thing for him, things would return to the way they were before.

Only to realize how foolish we had been in not accepting that the relationship had never been like that. I knew it. You knew it. Everybody that has ever been in a bad relationship knows it. Michael was always like this, he has always used you, and you just chose not to see it. Instead, you wanted him to, at last, be your "Prince Charming," so you could finally say the search is over and start making wedding plans, ha!

I stared at him through blurred vision, over wispy white faux fur, and thought, *Well, sweetheart, here's your prince.* The unfortunate part that angered me the most about this was that being in this situation was something I had gone through before. In fact, this situation was so dejavu-ish that I half caught me wondering if, somehow, I hadn't accidentally crossed that invisible line bordering my realm and the *twilight zone.*

I looked at Michael, eyes the same color as the ocean I loved so much, hair the color of wheat, slightly crooked smile when he laughed. I imagined how I looked, caramel skinned, full lips, brown eyes; our baby would have been beautiful. But I knew I was as ready to have a child as Eminem was prepared to stop pissing people off with his music. I didn't have the resources, and Michael would be okay at first, but down the line, his feelings would turn to hatred eventually and hatred for the child.

I cried harder. I hated myself so badly at that moment for my decision. Seven years ago, I made this same decision, and I still couldn't get it out of my mind. Seven years ago, I promised myself I would never endure this again. Seven years ago ... I buried my face into the back of Remy's furry head. I wanted to die.

"Make the call," I finally said.

For a moment, he must not have believed what I had said. But, then, he just lay there looking at me as if trying to be sure, but not saying anything for fear that his words would anger me and I would change my mind out of spite.

"Call the fucking clinic, Michael!" I screamed.

Chapter XV

I don't hate you; I only hate the devil inside you...

I could feel each beat from my heart inside my head. The echo of the sound bounced around inside the cavern of my skull a million times, it seemed before the next beat sounded. But, of course, this is to be expected when you spend the whole damn day drinking, crying, and not eating. Not that I didn't feel like I deserved this, but the pain is still pain.

Michael had moved to his perch on the patio to speak to Stacey, the nurse at the clinic, and smoke and make life-altering decisions for me since I had relented power over this problem to him. I could hear every word of his mouth through the thin glass panes separating the bedroom from the patio. I wished I could go deaf with each exhalation and inhalation of breath he took.

I didn't want to be part of it, I told myself. I already knew the psychological nightmare that would follow. The test, the touching, the probing, everything I knew I would have to face alone. These thoughts, among others, chased the heartbeats bouncing around in my head at the speed of light. So fast, I suddenly felt like they would accomplish what my prayers to the Almighty hadn't.

Lying there, I decided that death by cranial combustion was too quick of an end for me. No, I deserved much worse for my decision to kill my fetus. But, even something in Nazi surgical research, I knew, wouldn't have been painful enough to appease my heart in this self-deprecating mood.

I wondered what time it was. Blinking through fuzzy faux fur that clung to my face, I rolled over to see the dial on the black Sony digital alarm clock/radio. The faceplate read 3:40 P.M. Somehow, I had expected it to be much later with everything that had happened so far. Guessing time really didn't fly when you were not having fun. I rolled back over and kept going with the stuffed bear in one hand.

I reached the end of the bed and tried to stand up but fell. Luckily, I landed on my knees, perfectly cushioned by the carpeted floor. I reached out for the side of the bed and used the side of the metal frame to pull myself up.

The movement sent the pain from the headache into overload, and my knees gave a little while I almost passed out. I held Remy tighter and took a deep breath to slow my heartbeat. Slowly, I released it from my lungs while trying hard to stay calm and relaxed. I decided to go to the bathroom for aspirin when I thought better of it, deciding that I hadn't suffered enough for my sins yet. I resolved to continue with this mentally numbing headache until further notice. Lugging Remy in tow like Linus' security blanket from the comic strip "Peanuts," I moved from the bedroom to the living room.

I stood in the hallway that opened into the living/dining room. Staring around from the hall entrance. It was as if I were looking at the place for the first time. In the corner, the computer desk we had picked from Office Depot glowed from the sunlight bouncing off the glass and silvery metal body. The light reflected onto the ceiling, walls, and all other surfaces within reach.

The effect was beautiful in its simplicity, yet I saw it as alien. Unlike us, its surface had remained unchanged since we bought it. I wish to be an inanimate object, to stay beautiful and unfeeling for all time. I moved from the hall to the area behind the front door in four steps, sliding down the doorframe onto the floor. I sat next to the woven beach bag I had left there earlier. With one arm wrapped around Remy, I reached inside and removed the journal.

I was exhausted because of my emotional day or the large consumption of beer. I did not feel like getting up. However, my present position on the floor felt extremely comfortable. I intended to just retrieve the notebook and then move to the couch. But now, those intentions were a thing of the past. I found a pen, opened the journal to the page where my story had left off earlier, and continued...

Sean was handsome, a trait that all the men in my life seemed to share. However, who could blame me? No one went out wanting to end up with the ugly guy. However, standing six feet tall, with broad shoulders, a narrow waist, rock-hard abs, and a spectacular smile, he would be the one whose looks haunted me to this day.

The first night we met, his smile, more than anything, proved to be the beginning of my undoing. Sean had a smile so beautiful in the concept that it should have belonged to heavenly deities. But instead, Lucifer had somehow stolen the secret from God and used it for his demonic princes to talk poor fools into signing over their souls for what they thought love was. Sean was one of those princes, unbeknownst to me. At least now, that's how I partially feel.

My single-parent mother had gone out of her way to protect me from myself at a young age. It is common for parents to protect their children from making the same mistakes as they did. It's even more common for children to go out of their way to do everything in their power to make those mistakes. Maybe it's an unspoken law in nature. Whatever the cause, at fifteen, I went behind my mother's back, and following Gloria's tutelage, I started "dating" Sean.

The first of many guys that my mother would disapprove of. I guess I could blame my stupidity on my nature and not nurture. By this time, my mom didn't mind me hanging with friends once my chores were done as long as I was outside in front of the house and she could see me or at Gloria's home, where she could drive by and check.

When Sean started hanging outside with us, I don't think my mom thought anything of it. After all, I was more into sports than my brothers were, and I read everything when I wasn't playing ball.

Lenard and Lee, always willing participants in any games I could devise to occupy our empty periods, welcomed Sean into our small circle. While all the time keeping a close eye on him. Lee liked that he had another guy the same age as him to hang out with. Lenard was not so thrilled. Len had reservations regarding the boy he thought was not good enough for me.

I, however, was fascinated with him. He was not too strong with his emotions or too weak. He was an ear for my troubles and dreams, plus arms to wrap around me at dusk on my way home from Gloria's house. He made me feel pretty, wanted, and intelligent like no one else did, and I was thankful beyond understanding.

He stopped two weeks after we started "dating" while walking me home from the school bus. I stopped and turned to look at him and see why the sudden halt in our travels. He looked down at me like it was the first time he had seen me. Then, reaching up with both hands, he cupped my face and kissed me.

I had been kissed before, nothing special, just a peck by Eric one day when he walked me to class. That afternoon when Sean kissed me, I lost my breath. My heart beat so fast that that's all I heard for a while, and time stood still. I dug my hands so far into my jeans pockets that I could have retired my shoelaces. When he finally stopped kissing me, momentarily, I became mummified by his power. He stepped away, leaving me for a split second too long. It was only after I heard him clear his throat was the spell broke.

He continued looking down at me like I should say something. I had nothing to say. My emotions were in turmoil. I just turned and started walking home a little too fast while trying to pretend that nothing had happened out of the ordinary. We continued our journey to my house, him with this stupid cat that ate the canary grin on his face and me mumbling about absolutely nothing the rest of the way home. When we got there, I hauled ass into the house, not bothering to stop and say hi to Len, who was with his dog outside.

That next day while conversing with Gloria on the phone, she brought up the subject of skipping school. I was terrified but agreed since I was tired of everyone calling me a goodie two shoes. We met at the bus stop as usual. Gloria told Laneika what was happening and told her to wait for us after the bus dropped her home so we could all walk home together so our parents would not be the wiser. She was so against it, and that little voice told me I should listen to her. However, we eventually gave in to Gloria's wishes and followed the plan.

It was 6:30 AM when we got to Ken's family house; they lived within walking distance from us. No one was home except us; his mom had died from cancer when he was very young, and his dad worked almost all the time. When we *got there, the sun still had not risen to its full glory, and we all just hung out in the living room watching early morning cartoons, eating, and conversing about nonsense. Everyone was very relaxed except me.*

I was confident we would be caught. Gloria reassured me that would not be the case and that, unknown to me, she had done this before, and I never figured it out. I was dumbfounded but agreed I would try to relax. Slowly, as the morning went on, Ken and she made their way to his room, leaving Sean and me alone in the living room. I stayed where I was on the couch; I was so nervous I had to use the bathroom every few minutes. He did not know what he thought would happen and hated Gloria for leaving me alone. I just wanted to go home.

I had no idea what to expect when Sean came and sat next to me. Making sure that my attention was on the television in front of me, I did not see when he picked up the decorative pillow until it was too late. The hit almost made me fall off the couch. As I regained my composure, another hit sent me completely over, and his laughter started. I rolled over on the floor, reached for the first pillow, and thumped him so he would stop smiling.

Before I knew it, we were in a full-blown pillow fight, each smacking the other in the head and torso. Soon I was being pounded so hard that I gave up on the pillow and tried to shove him away from me. He retaliated by grabbing my arms. I twisted and tried to free myself from his grip. Then, very gently, he moved forward quickly and, using a karate move, swiped my legs from under me, causing both of us to fall onto the red shag carpet.

We lay there laughing for a while. I stared into his warm brown eyes, feeling the expansion and contraction of his lungs as he breathed. His legs mingled with mine. He stared down at me as he used one arm to prop himself up and the other to move some displaced hair off his face. Then, slowly, his face moved down toward mine till soon he was just centimeters from mine.

I could smell his sweet breath as his fingertips moved from my face to my arms. Then, leisurely, he moved closer till our lips touched. I stiffened from the initial contact but slowly relaxed as his lips pressed against mine. Finally, his tongue softly spread my lips apart and slid into my mouth.

I reached up with both hands and encircled his neck with my arms. We had stayed for what seemed like an eternity. Then, he smoothly moved the arm he had used to prop himself up under my head while simultaneously pulling me closer to him. I exhaled from the movement. My body felt weak and alive at the same time in his arms.

He moved his lips away from mine and across my cheeks, only to kiss them briefly. He lightly bit the tip of my earring-less earlobe, causing a current of electricity to move down my spine from my cheeks to my ear. My legs moved up towards his crotch without my control. My spine curved up involuntarily closer to him as he moved from my ear to my neck; he suckled on that large portion of my skin as if he were dying of hunger, and the mere act of sucking on my flesh would sustain his life.

I moaned, realizing that this was not something I was comfortable with and that all this was happening too fast. I tried to push him away, but he grabbed my arms and pinned them above my head as he kissed my lips. Slowly, again I relaxed. Crossing my arm together, he held both above my head with only one of his hands. With his free hand, he moved down the side of my body, over my stomach, and into my pants.

I froze. I didn't know what to do. Every single instance my mother called me "whore" went through my mind in that one second that afternoon. Finally, I pulled my arms from where they had been pinned and ripped his hand from inside my pants. He moved to the side and apologized if he had offended me. I said nothing, just stood up and ran to the bathroom.

I stayed on the tub's rim for an hour; he never came to check on me. When finally, I found the courage again to go outside. I found him lying on the sofa with two unopened condoms on the coffee table beside him. I was furious. What the hell did he think was going to happen? I didn't even know him like that. As soon as I confronted him, his face turned puzzled, as if I was the ignorant one and had no right to come at him like that.

Angered even more by his disposition, I went straight to Ken's door, banged on it until I got Gloria's attention, and insisted we go home. Fifteen minutes later, Ken finally stepped out. Gloria was on the bed underneath the covers. As far as I could tell, she was dressed.

I ran to her crying, and she hugged me and told me it was okay. I told her I wanted to go home. I didn't care if I got in trouble. She said it was okay Ken would take care of it. Thirty minutes after *my first adolescent breakdown, I heard the front door close. Ken came in and announced that Sean had left. He said he would call me later. . . he never did that day. The next time I saw him was a week later. I was outside hanging out with Lee. He came walking up to us like the first night we met and informed me he needed to talk to me . . .*

Michael came walking in from the patio as calm as a Buddhist priest straight from meditation. He looked around and spotted me staring back at him over the top of my journal. I felt like a schoolgirl looking up at her teacher in class. He walked straight to my side, picked up Remy, and sat on the floor next to me under the kitchen counter area. I closed the journal on my lap and turned to look into his eyes.

He stretched out his arms and invited me into his embrace. I was either not thinking straight or feeling incredibly alone. Whichever, I fell into his arms, only wanting the warmth of another person close to me. Michael explained that

Stacey, the nurse with whom he had been on the phone, had made an appointment for me to go in tomorrow.

Tomorrow!

I groaned. Everything was moving too fast. I had hoped I would have a few days to prepare mentally for this. However, it appeared that it was only a dream within this nightmare. He continued about the procedure and what the nurse recommended. All I thought about now was, Should I do this? How safe was it for my body to go through this again?

"She says there are two procedures you can choose from, a surgical one and a non-surgical —one—"

"Which one is safer, Mike?" I interrupted." Which one won't mess me up? Did you ask her that?" I started to get up, and the journal fell off my lap. His hand reached out and restrained me. I struggled, but he was more potent and pulled me down on top of him. Our faces were too close. I turned away from him.

"No, I didn't," he whispered in my ear. "But I will, baby. You know I only want what's best for you. I love you so much. You can talk to her too if you want. She sounds like a very nice woman." He moved one of my braids off my face and around my ear, then kissed me on the side of my neck.

"No, I don't want to." I adjusted myself into a comfortable sitting position on his lap. I began to cry again. He wrapped his arms around me, pulling me closer to his chest. The rhythm of his heart pulsated through me. I closed my eyes and allowed the tears to flow in silence down my face. We sat there for a while. Michael rocked me back and forth like the baby we would never have.

As gentle as any summer breeze on a hot day, he kissed my neck again. I trembled and turned to look at him. Our eyes locked for a moment too long, and he kissed me. I let him. I needed it, and I wanted it. However, it became apparent that his constant presence was more harmful than helpful. Nonetheless, I felt like he was all I had. The best I had in all the evil around me.

I kissed him back harder, our tongues intertwined, each fighting to control the other's mouth. Kissing turned into touching, fingers probing, digging into flesh and muscle. Then, feeling something else, before I could stop myself, my shirt was over my head, and my legs were wrapped around him like a champion jockey. I could feel his rigid pulsing member under me, between my legs, thin layers of clothing keeping it apart. His hands moved the cups of my bra aside, and his mouth greedily encompassed my nipples one at a time.

I pushed him back and pulled off both layers of his shirt before thrusting my tongue deeper into his throat. I dug my nails into his back without bothering to hold back any strength, wanting him in pain, wanting him to bleed. A gasp escaped him. He grabbed me by my hair and pulled me back, exposing my neck just enough for him to envelope it with his lips. This, too, he sucked selfishly like a vampire on a feeding frenzy. I wanted him so bad, and as if he was reading my mind, he stood with me still wrapped around his waist like a serpent.

He moved me to the sofa, removing my pants and thong. With my back arched in a position no chiropractor would recommend, he spread my legs and dived his face into the pink center. I moaned, grabbed two hands full of his golden locks, and shoved his lips and face further. That day when we had sex, it was not soft or gentle in the least.

On the contrary, it was rough and violent, like we were taking the pain of our emotional problems out on each other's physical being. In my mind, at this moment, I knew that I did not love him. It was now and had always been lust that I felt for him, but how good did the desire feel at that time when he finally stopped teasing me with his tongue and fucked me as I had begged him to do?

Chapter XVI

History repeats itself...

The doctor's office was so uncomfortable. It was probably the cause of most of his patient's physical suffering, if not their actual pain. The burgundy vinyl padded chairs were stiff, challenging, and unrelenting. The temperature in the room felt like it was in the mid-30s. The cheery "made for office" painting annoyed me and made me feel like I was the worst person for my decision. The tears would not cease running down my face and ruining my makeup.

Directly across from Mike and me, a petite brunette sat quietly in a two-piece resembling an Ann Taylor suit, buying time by rearranging things on her Palm Pilot. She was alone, for all I could make out, and now and then, she would glimpse up at me with a frown. This only caused me to feel even worst. That was supposed to be me, I thought. Calm, cool, and collected. I had made this decision, no one else, I reminded myself. So why in the hell was I acting like a big baby?

Michael, however, played his part superbly. He was attentive and caring, whispering loving and seemingly sincere words whenever possible. He even wiped the tears from my face and brought more tissue from the corner table next to the magazine rack, so I wouldn't have to move too much.

Michael looked like he cared about the outside world, but I knew better.

I finished the two-inch thick pile of medical forms and walked up to the crystallized glass window that parted the inner office from the patient lobby. I rang the electric bell that seemed to come as standard equipment in all doctors' offices. The nurse slid the glass partition to the side, revealing a glimpse of the office beyond my immediate domain. Unfortunately, it was just as assaulting the senses as the one behind me. Cold, sterile, "medicated," and trying too hard to be cheery with its made-to-order happy people paintings.

The nurses, however, more than made up for the insensitive accommodations. They appeared genuine in their concern, solemn, and endearing due to the nature of their work. The redhead behind the glass retrieved the clipboard from my hands and directed me to sit back down. I rejoined Michael in the waiting room with the pretty brown-haired woman. On top of everything I was going through, I was starving.

I hadn't eaten since last night, and my stomach would have been empty if it was not for a 32-oz bottle of Zephyr Hills; I had chugged it down before coming into the office following the doctor's demands for the ultra-sound to drink plenty of fluids before the exam. Trying to look at the glass half-full, I pondered that my bladder was complete, even if my stomach was empty.

After what seemed like an eternity of positioned there festering in self-loathing and envy of the brunette seated across from us, a pleasant blond woman wearing colorful scrubs and a made-for-TV smile came through the door that connected the two rooms together and called my name. I stood up, placing the magazine on my lap on the chair. Michael stood almost instantly. I walked toward her, wiping the last evidence of pain and reluctance on my sleeve.

"Ms. Pierre?" she said, looking at me with unsure eyes as I approached her.

I nodded. She asked me to follow her into the inner chambers of the office. Then, seeing Michael at my heels, she paused.

"I'm sorry." She looked inquisitively at Michael. "Are you Mr. Pierre?"

"No," I answered before he had a chance to. "He's just a friend of mine."

The nurse looked at him and then at me. "Would you like him to wait outside for you?"

I looked at her and shook my head in affirmation. "Yes, I would rather him not join me," I said, preferring not to have Michael there since his perfect boyfriend act was on my last nerve. The nurse returned to the doorway we had just left. Letting the door fall open next to her, she indicated that he should return to his seat in the outer office.

One corridor led to the next hallway, which went around a corner to another passage. Each led past doors with patient charts held up high by a transparent container. Door after door was closed from prying eyes, occupied probably with women under the same mental self-inquisition I was putting myself through. Probably coming up with just as little of a good answer for the many questions that plagued them about why exactly they were here.

We finally arrived at a door with a large golden number six stenciled. I wondered where the other two sixes were that would truly signify what I was doing here was the devil's work and that I would forever rot in hell. I almost laughed out loud, thinking my place there was not already assured. She led me into a small sitting room and asked me to sit. She sat across from me and opened my chart on her lap.

"Ms. Pierre, my name is Sam," said the nurse. A pain shot through my heart as I remembered the pain the last woman in my life, Sam, had caused me. The discomfort that her name brought me must have shown on my face because she paused in the introduction to ask me if I was okay.

"Yes, I'm fine," I responded

"Good. Then we can begin. I'm the counselor here. It's my job to go through the whole procedure with you so that you feel comfortable...." She paused to allow me to speak while she flipped through the pages.

I said nothing. She tapped absent-mindedly with a black pen on my patient chart on her lap.

"Is this your first time having this procedure done?" she asked.

"Yes," I lied

"Our facility specializes in this type of procedure. I want you to know you are in good hands. Patient confidentiality is paramount to us, and so is a safe, trauma-free recovery." Again, she looked up at me. I simply nodded to indicate she should continue her monologue.

"The doctor will ask you to undress from the waist down, then to lie on a gynecological examining bed. He will give you a mask connected directly to an O2 tank. This will be your sedative. With every breath you take, the effect will be stronger, making you feel light-headed and numb. There is no actual cutting involved in the process, only a tube inserted into your vaginal canal. The tubes act in the same method as a vacuum. There will be a slight pressure in your lower abdomen and the feeling of suction. You will not be in pain or conscious of what is happening...."

"At least, not physically," I said out loud, not meaning to.

Sam stopped, closed the file on her lap, and looked at me. She gave me one of those "let's be friends" looks that nurses had to practice a dozen times before they left the house every day.

She proceeded with the question that I knew was coming.

"Selene ... are you being pressured into this decision? I mean, you know there are other alternatives you can consider besides an early termination of the pregnancy, right?"

"Yes, Sam, I know this. This is my decision."

"I see. Well okay. Your boyfriend is welcome to join you in the recovery room, but not during the. "Procedure."

"He's not my boyfriend. He's just a ... friend."

"Well," She cleared her throat. "Your friend then." She finished the monologue.

I signed the remainder of the paperwork Sam handed me.

As if reading my mind or seeing the need in my eyes, she said, "You must really need to use the bathroom right now."

"You have no idea," I said, favoring her with a small smile.

"Well, it will be just a minute until the doctor performs the ultrasound, and then you can go to the bathroom."

Sam stood up and opened the door, so I could precede her. She walked out of the small inner seating room and turned to let me know by her direction where to go next. However, before she could direct me, a curvaceous brown-haired woman, also in colorful scrubs, walked up to Sam and took possession of my chart.

"Hi, I'm Stacey. Please follow me."

Not waiting for a response, she moved ahead of me and walked around the corner. I followed, half-conscious of what was going on. The hall was filled with women and nurses, all lost in their worlds, thoughts, and hurts. I was only a grain of sand on the beach, waiting to be moved to a better place by a strong wave.

Chapter XVII

Alone in a room full of people...

I half undressed underwear, jeans, and socks. Folded everything into a neat little pile and placed the pile on the single chair in the corner of the room. Climbing the single step unto the examining table, I sat at the edge with the semi-towel-like cover Stacey had given draped over my body's lower half. I began the tedious yet exhausting process of waiting on the doctor.

Lost in my thoughts, I began to reflect on life and my life.

I thought about the sixteen-year-old girl I used to be, the one that had known so clearly that even though Prince Charming was not real, love was, and nobody ever had to settle for less just because they were scared of being alone.

I thought about how that fear had gotten the best of me a year after Mrs. J's death when I had found my mother alone in the dark kitchen crying to herself, with no one to hold her. My mother, the fearless woman who used verbal assaults when reprimanding me for making me stronger, had looked so weak standing over the kitchen sink with silent sobs rocking her body.

I thought about how I had wanted to go to her, to hold her and let her know whatever it was, it would be okay, but I hadn't out of fear. Fear of her reaction to the invasion of her privacy, of me seeing her at such a weak moment. So instead, I snuck back into my room and silently swore to myself that I would never be alone. I would have a faithful husband who loved me as much as I loved him. That I would not reprimand my children, with them always knowing that I loved them and that although my life would never be a fairy tale, it would be as close to perfect as possible.

I felt a tear run down my face from the overwhelming emotions, realizing that maybe the fact that I had seen my mother that night in such a vulnerable position had changed something inside me. Something that had driven me into a frantic search not to be alone.

I thought about how I hated waiting on anything by myself because it gave me too much time to think about life and how one of the body's most significant reactions to the mind is during the process of waiting, waiting for a birth, death, surgery, sleep, fulfillment, freedom, acknowledgment, love, lust and/or money. Our muscles tighten, stomachs churn, agitation sets in, we become fidgety, irritated, and angry, and then it all converts to fear.

No one, I suppose, could take pleasure in anything going on around them until the waiting was over, until the answer for the reason they were waiting was found. Nonetheless, for the time it takes for this knowledge to be bestowed upon us until we know, we mentally wait.

Therefore, we physically pay. I stared at my feet, physically cold, emotionally and physically alone, wanting desperately not to feel the ills of waiting.

My thoughts drifted to seven years ago when I had found myself in a room like this, going through almost exactly this, promising myself that this would never happen again. How stupid could I have been to let myself fall into the same trap as before? A fool, I was, a child in a woman's body, wishing and hoping each new relationship would be the love of my life that I had always wanted and promised myself I would have.

Snap out of it, I thought. Self-loathing was not accomplishing anything except for maybe more emotional deterioration.

As I pulled the covering higher on my legs and attempted to tuck it around my thigh to keep me a bit warmer, I realized that I had just answered the question about why I had started going from one relationship to another, looking for Mister right. By not wanting to be alone and ending up like my mother with a whole bunch of kids and no one to comfort me when I cried, I had unconsciously done this to myself. However, this insight did not answer why I had let myself fall into these relationship woes, loving others more than they loved me.

I glanced at my purse sitting on the stool in front of me. I wondered if I had enough time to grab it and write down some of the things that were floating in my mind regarding my current relationship and how I believed I had gotten there when Stacey walked in, suddenly followed by the doctor. Their appearance chased away the phantoms of my past that had kept me company in the subzero-like room.

The doctor was going gray. More precisely, he was gray with an undertone of darkness to his hairline, six feet one inch, about two hundred pounds, with blue scrubs that fit his mid-section too snuggly. He was not in good shape, though as a doctor, I would think he should be. He introduced himself but never looked at me nor shook my hand, which I had extended to him. Instead, he patted me on the back and avoided my touch as if I were a leper. He could not afford the kind of humane contact. As if to do so would make him more part of the wrong he was being paid to correct.

He had the worst bedside manner I had ever endured, and I've suffered a lot. I watched him ignore me. And suddenly I wanted to scream: "Look at me, asshole, I'm a person, too. I am young. Yes, I am stupid. I am scared, but I did not deserve this treatment!" However, I did not give voice to my thoughts; I simply lay back as Stacey instructed and tried to blink away the tears as the nurse started the procedure for the sonogram.

Stacey poured a gel-like substance on my lower abdomen, which was even colder than the room, and gently spread it over my lower half. The doctor stood over me and still refused to look me in the face. Then, finally, he recovered from Stacey what looked like a white plastic stirring spoon with a flat tip. He placed the instrument on my lower abdomen and began pressing it down firmly, moving it back and forth, then up and down.

It didn't hurt, but my bladder was packed, and I felt I would piss on myself if he pushed down any harder. Instead, the doctor proved I was again wrong about something else by pressing down harder the second time. The doctor continued his predetermined route across my lower abs, not acknowledging my discomfort.

"Either she's too early or not pregnant because I can't find it ..." he exclaimed to the nurse with the emotions of a Petri dish. Then, he stopped the pressure on my stomach.

"Stacey, please prep her for a V.S.," he said as he removed his gloves, threw them in the hazardous waste basket, and walked out of the room, still not bothering to say anything to me.

I sat up before I was instructed. I wondered if the hope now in my head from the doctor's words was evident on my face. Pulling the cover higher to conceal myself, my mind still tried to digest exactly what the doctor's words meant. But I dared not live in those thoughts for too long. So instead, I spoke what I could.

"Ma'am, may I use the bathroom now?" I asked while wiping the gooey mess off my stomach with Stacey's paper towel.

Stacey looked up at me with piercing green eyes. I half-expected to be part of some psychic revelation from her gaze, but there was none. Instead, she looked away and returned everything in the room to its proper place. She removed a plastic specimen cup from one of the drawers, turned around, and handed it to me.

"Yes, sweetheart, but I need you to fill this cup so we can take another pregnancy test for you, okay?"

Stacey placed the cup next to me as I finished getting dressed. Ten minutes later, the stupid cup was filled and handed to another nurse waiting for me when I exited the bathroom. My guess was, by now, Stacey, with her emerald green eyes, was already repeating her previous action with yet another girl who had found herself in this particular predicament, being treated like dirt from under Dr. Moreau's shoe.

My mood hadn't improved. I was still starving but no longer in danger of pissing on myself. Not having anyone to direct me to where I was supposed to be, I took up a British Castle guard post next to a wall. I heard sniffling and saw Sam leading a young woman to her office. She looked as distraught as I had been less than an hour ago.

I wish I could honestly say I knew what she was going through, but that would be a lie and an overestimation of my powers of deduction when it came to these situations. Therefore, with sympathy in my heart for her pain, I took a deep breath and looked away around the labyrinth of examining rooms and corridors.

The pro-choice center was packed. So busy, I started wondering how profitable it must be for a doctor involved in this business. Moreover, why did the prick doctor feel he did not have to show sympathy toward his patients? I mean, you estimate if most women were here for the same reason as mine, they were spending about $450 a procedure, and from the look of all the people around me, there were at least twelve women here, including myself and excluding staff.

I asked one of the nurses for a pen as I stood next to a wall. And did the math in the palm of my hand. A smile of amazement came to me as I saw the sum I had reached, 5,400 dollars in two hours! But, of course, that did not include expenses.

Nevertheless, by my calculation and my guess, rarely do doctors in this business need a loan for their newest Benz purchase. No wonder my doctor treated his patients the way he did. I wondered if he had a daughter or had any idea of what the emotional pressure was like for a woman going through this. I asked whether he cared. Then, a quote from M.L.K. Jr. came into my head:

"Our scientific power has outrun our spiritual power. As a result, we have guided missiles and misguided men."

I guess the same could be said of the women, including myself, that felt like this was their only choice. A cold that had nothing to do with the air conditioning system ran down the back of my neck, causing the thin brown hairs that occupied that space to stand on end. I had to ask myself again. Why was I doing this?

Stacey found me there, lost in my thoughts, standing in front of the corner, trying to become one with the drywall.

"Sweetheart ..."

I looked up. The nurse smiled curtly, trying to reassure me.

"Please come with me," she said as she turned for me to follow her into the next room.

Once I was again sitting on a new examination table, she began. "According to the latest test results, you are pregnant ...."

I groaned as the last feeble ray of hope I had held in my subconscious dissipated.

"At this point, we will have to do a V.S., a vaginal scan. But, first, the doctor needs to determine how far along you are in the pregnancy to determine the best course of action."

I said nothing, just nodded my understanding while trying to rub out the math problem on my left palm. Then, finally, she turned to move and stopped as if something had compelled her to say more.

"Ms. Pierre, the doctor has asked me to apologize to his patients today for his less-than-personable attitude. He is facing some tribulations, and he is trying very hard to have it not to interfere with his work. Helping women is what he loves to do. However, you know that it can be hard to help others when we are facing problems."

I smiled, feeling a lot better. At least I did not cause the doctor to act as he had. I wondered why the doctor hadn't apologized, coming up with why men, even the doctor, had problems and apologized for their mistakes to the women in his life. This thought made me feel even better, knowing doctors were not immune to human problems.

The nurse continued out the door. I followed, silent as a mouse but much less heavy with fear. I was brought to another room, which could have been a clone of the last, except for the machinery. The same undressing series was conducted as in the previous test, and I lay down precisely as I had before.

The same doctor came in. Again, I expected the same robotic emotionless service from him. Except now, I understood where it was coming from.

"Ms. Pierre," he said. I looked up from my laying position on the bed.

"I just wanted to say not to be scared. Sometimes things happen to us that send our lives in an unexpected direction. You will be fine. My staff and I will take great care of you."

As he spoke, I noticed his eyes were red, as if he had been crying. I wondered what ailed him as he gave me a warm smile, handed the chart back to Stacey, and headed back to the other end of the table.

A tear ran down my face. *Sometimes things happen to us that send our lives in an unexpected direction,* I thought. Closing my eyes as he inserted the device into me, I was uncomfortable but not as scared as I might have been. As I lay there, I wondered what had happened to the doctor that had suddenly turned his frigid exterior so warm.

Had the problem he was facing resolved itself? Had he encountered someone who reminded him that he was there to make us feel better and not to mope around while taking our money? Or had he realized that sometimes things happened that sent our lives in an unexpected direction?

The scan was performed.

He reassured me as much as he thought was necessary. Trying harder than what I thought was normal for him to put me at ease. Stacey sat at the controls, a small smile playing on her face. She seemed clearly pleased with herself with the amount of empathy Dr. Moreau was showing to me. He said something to the nurse too low for me to hear, took the instrument out, stood up, threw his gloves in the hazardous waste basket, and before he walked out, he reminded me that I was in good care, and I, in turn, thanked him.

He smiled and walked out.

I sat up and closed my legs. Now, if I could remember to do that when it came to my boyfriends, I wouldn't be in this mess.

"Sweetheart, you can get dressed now. Come outside so Sam can talk to you when you're done." With that, she walked out of the room.

I finished getting dressed for the third time today since I woke up. Walking out of the room, Stacey was waiting for me.

"Sweetheart ..."

I was beginning to believe that her favorite adjective for all persons, like mine was "babe." Whatever happened to call people by their birth names, I wondered?

"You are only about four weeks into this pregnancy right now. When I was on the phone with your boyfriend yesterday …."

I rolled my eyes, not even bothering to correct the title the nurse was still bestowing on Mike.

"I told him to schedule the appointment for next week, but he insisted on today…"

I stood there thinking to myself that I was not the least bit surprised. He would want to have this behind him as soon as possible, so I could move out.

"Anyway, Sam will soon discuss your options with you. Maybe you want to go outside and get some air. "

I shook my head yes and used the door the nurse indicated to the rear of the front desk to exit the inner office.

The office building in which the doctor's office was located was a two-story high complex wrapped around a rectangular open courtyard with a large palm tree in the middle. To either side of the tree were staircases that led up to the second-floor offices. A young couple was sitting on a green bench directly under the tree. It could have been a scene from any park in America if they were not so close to the clinic.

Michael was nowhere to be found from my first scan of the courtyard. I re-entered the office using the door that led to the lobby, even though I already knew he was not there. A blond couple had replaced the pretty brunette, but dear old Michael wasn't there either. I returned outside. I did not want to intrude on the couple on the bench, so I sat on the staircase facing the parking lot.

What should I have expected from him, to hang around and wait for me like he cared? No, I knew better. For all he knew, I was deep into the "surgery" by now.

I was there less than five minutes when he came walking up from the direction I was facing. I guess he had been in the car. He was going to go right past me and into the office, but my whistling got his attention. He pulled the tennis cap off his head. His blond hair fell and scattered. He hadn't had time to spend his usual half-hour in the mirror this morning attending to its every strand.

"Hey, what are you doing out here?" I moved over so he could sit down next to me. "Did you change your mind or something?" he said nervously.

"Yup, I'm going to keep it," I said.

"Really?"

I looked at him awhile, wanting him to stew in anxiety.

"No, not really. I'm too early for the procedure." I turned to face him. "The nurse said she had advised you that next week would probably be better for me, but you insisted on today. Why would you do that? Didn't you think the extra time would have been good for me to emotionally deal with this, to digest the decision I had made to terminate a life?"

"Well, I wanted to be there for you, and I didn't know if I was going to be able to get next week off." He tried to sound sincere, but the faux emotion was like nails on a chalkboard in my ears.

He was lying, and I knew it. He couldn't even look me in the eyes and kept playing with his watch. I was just about to say something when I heard my name being called.

We both looked up simultaneously to see Sam looking back at me. I started to get up, and so did he.

"Can I come in this time?" he asked.

"As long as it's okay with Sam. I don't care much what you do, Mike." With that, I walked back into the office.

We followed her to her office. She sat us down and shook Mike's hand since it was the first time they were actually meeting. Before she could open her mouth, he asked, "So what can we do today, Sam, so that Selene doesn't have to go through any more emotional turmoil?"

I fixed him a look that said, 'Shut up, or God help you, you will see the island come out of me in the middle of all these nice white folks.'

"You still have two options, Selene; the first is that you can try the new pill on the market, Mifepristone or RU-486. I don't know if you have heard of it. It's being called the abortion pill. The second is to wait for next week and return, and we can proceed with the surgical procedure."

"Pill?" My eyebrow was doing 'The Rock's signature one eyebrow raised in confusion stare.

"Yes, it's a series you take over forty-eight hours."

"Really?" Michael responded, seeming happier by the minute for the sudden unexpected prospect.

"Yes, the chemical breaks down the tissue of the embryo sack and allows her body to reject the pregnancy, much like a miscarriage."

I groaned. I had been through a miscarriage before, which was not the most painless thing in the world. Nevertheless, I continued to bestow upon Sam 'The Rock's signature stare. Michael sat next to her. I could feel the relief from this option spewing from him, like sweat on a hot summer's day.

"Is it painful?" I asked.

Michael responded before Sam could, "Of course not, Selene. They wouldn't recommend anything that would hurt you."

Sam and I looked at him, trying to determine what he thought he knew to make that statement.

"Actually," Sam continued, "It is somewhat painful, sort of like menstrual cramps, but about three times worse."

"See, baby girl, like a cramp, you deal with those all the time."

Staring at him through slanted eyes and clinched teeth, I managed to get out, "I don't get cramps, Mike and my friends who do are in serious pain the whole time, and she just said three times worse!" I said, indicating Sam.

"But babe, you're stronger than all your friends, and I'm sure this won't hurt as much to you."

"What the fuck is that supposed to mean?"

Sam didn't give him a chance to bury himself any more than he already had but came to his rescue. I guess she was trying to defuse the situation and calm me down.

"Ms. Pierre, we will prescribe you an extreme pain reliever."

"Yeah."

"Yes, and it is 99.9 % safe, so you don't have to worry about anything. And if you feel in danger at any time during the process, we have a twenty-four-hour number, and you can always go to a hospital."

"See, babe."

I glared at him, daring him to say one more word. But, instead, he swallowed anything more he had to say and shut up.

"Okay," Sam continued. "The procedure is simple. If you decide to go with that option, what happens is that you take one pill now before you leave the office. Then after the next thirty-six hours, you'll insert four of them with a plunger into your vaginal canal. It's all straightforward; as I said before, we give you written instructions. I'll give you two some time to talk about it. I'll be right outside by the front desk when you two have come to a decision. "

As soon as Sam walked out of the office. Michael moved from the seat next to me to the one Sam had occupied before me. I was now staring at his face to face instead of having to turn to look at him.

"It doesn't sound like a bad idea; it sounds much better than you having surgery."

"Mike, have you ever had a cramp?" He shook his head no. "I didn't think so," I said, exhausted

"Babe, I want to be with you while you go through everything."

I sat there slumped in the chair, running both hands over my face and through my hair.

"And with me taking today off, I don't think I will be able to come with you if you decide to wait to come back next week. I know you're strong and may not need me there, but it would make me feel better to be with you while you're going through this."

I continued to say nothing. I just looked at Michael. Sam's words reverberated: *Like a cramp but about three times worse.*

I had never had a cramp before but had seen my friends endure them. My sister would get so sick she would vomit. But that was them. I was strong.

I was looking at Michael sitting across from me, not listening to the words coming out of his mouth. I was sure he was doing a perfect imitation of caring about me. But I was also contemplating that doing this whole non-surgical thing would allow him to be there for me when he might not be able to next week if he really wanted to be there. I knew I didn't want to be alone but was the best course of action relying on him for comfort?

I looked at Michael, really looked at him. He was nothing more than a slightly manipulative little jerk. Not a person that I should want to always have a piece of my heart or a person I should hope to have an understanding of the emotional pain I was going through. Instead, I had to know that all he did was for himself and not rely on him for reassurance. He was calculating and selfish, just like his dad.

Like father, like spawn, I thought.

"Selle, are you listening to me?"

"Huh?"

"I was just saying ...."

I got up from the chair and headed for the door. Michael grabbed hold of my wrist

"Where are you going?"

"To tell Sam my decision," I spat out while twisting my arm free of his hold.

"What are you going to do?" His blue eyes were so anxious that I wondered what his blood pressure reading would have said if I had taken it right then.

"I am going to take the pill, Michael, but not for you, for me. I can't keep going like this. Something has to change; I have to change. I have to start taking control of my life, and I can't do that with a baby," I finished while opening the door.

He followed me.

"Okay, but don't worry about anything. I will be there for you. I know my words have not meant shit lately, but I mean this. I'm going to take care of you."

I said nothing. I just kept walking toward the front desk, toward Sam, toward yet another chapter in my life. I did not know if he was lying to make himself feel better by saying that or what. Nevertheless, I was not buying it.

Chapter XVIII

We all wear a mask to hide from the world...

As I left the doctor's office, prescription in hand and belly full of medication that would allow my body to reject what was naturally growing within it, I took the first step to exit the office, and my vision seemed to adjust. My pupils dilated, my hearing sharpened, and I saw the world anew. I wondered if it was an effect of the medication or something else. As I walked to the car, I thought, here I was, willingly killing a part of me. Not as fast as I had initially planned, but slowly and intently, and for what?

I turned to look at Mike. He looked odd, like he wasn't real, just the lingering shadow of a bad dream reminiscent of a foolish memory. I pondered if I was finally losing it mentally from the trauma I had caused myself over the years. Or if my mind, having been so traumatized, had been forced to evolve to survive. Forced physical evolution is the most common type of science, so why not a forced mental evolution.

It was a disturbing new outlook on my mental prowess, yet I somehow found myself comforted. I wanted to believe that though I didn't think myself to be a fighter anymore, at least I was not as much of one as I had been when I was younger, that my subconscious would override my conscious mind to save itself and thus save me in the process.

I got into the car and sat down without paying much attention to anything around me. Instead, my mind drifted through the day's events as I stared at him on the drive home. I didn't know why. Maybe hoping my new gift of sight would somehow morph backward, back into the foolishness it was before. After all, isn't ignorance bliss? Perhaps I feared what awareness would bring me.

"I'm starving," he said while adjusting the cap on his head and looking in the rearview mirror.

I rolled my eyes at his apparent vanity. How could I have thought I loved this idiot? But his statement did bring up the crucial point of my empty (stomach?), which I had completely forgotten about. But with his mention of food, a grumble came from my abdomen to remind me.

"Me too. What are you buying us?" I said jokingly, trying my darkness to make light of a bad situation.

"I just spent almost five hundred dollars on that thing. Can't you pay?" Michael replied. Then, I turned to look at him to ensure he was not joking in suggesting that I should pay.

The words 'what a fucking asshole' were just about to come out of my mouth, but I bit my lower lip and asked what he wanted to eat. Chili's, what a fucking surprise. That place had been the first place we went to when I moved here. After that, there was practically one on every other corner in this town. Of course, there were great high-end restaurants, but if you just wanted someplace to get a bit to eat, Chili's seemed to be your only choice.

Not really wanting Chili's, but not wanting an argument, I resigned and called to be picked up. Deciding that the only thing to keep me from telling Michael exactly how I felt with all the colorful language that being pissed off brought out was to write. So, I reached into my purse and took out the journal.

He looked down at it for a split second.

"You have been writing into that thing a lot lately," he said, indicating the journal with a tilt of his head.

"Yup."

"What are you writing about?"

"Stuff."

"What kind of *stuff?*"

"I'm trying to figure out during which relationship I've had, did I decide that a guy like you, who doesn't really know what love is, was worth putting myself through all this shit for. When I narrow it down, I will be better at making the right decisions regarding guys."

He said nothing. I decided to quit while I was ahead. Then a thought occurred to me. Did I know what love was? Was I sitting there accusing him of being empty of love when I knew nothing? I flipped the journal almost to the back pages and wrote ....

What is this thing called love? The explanation eludes me. I had thought I knew once, but something happened again, which shattered those perceptions. Love cannot be what I keep thinking it is. I have done everything I thought would make the man I am in a relationship happy. Always going by the golden rule of treating them how I wished to be treated, to no avail.

It was like there was a missing ingredient in the recipe that would make my love life perfect. But I was missing it, and no matter how I wished, I could just walk into a grocery store and buy that missing ingredient like you do, egg and milk. But it was not that easy.

As I sat in that car writing that, an understanding came to me, and it was the most painful thing I had to accept so far. This realization hit me in the chest like a thousand-pound boulder rolling down a hill and falling on me unsuspectingly. It knocked the breath from inside my lungs, causing me to gasp for breath as I fought my body's urge to cry.

I had known that my Michael was a jerk, and over the last few months, I had begun to understand that he did not love me and had just been using me as arm candy to be shown off in his little all-white community as fuel to feed his ego. But it was not until then that I realized I was worthless to him. While I had positioned myself there polishing the pedestal, I had put Michael on. He sat up high, looking down at me. This thought of how he perceived me as nothing was devastating. The gifts I bought, the trips, and the ordeals we faced had all been lies.

Closing my mouth and breathing through my nose, I fought the urge to break down, punch the dashboard in front of me, and punch him. But, instead, I felt like I did that morning on the phone with Daniel; my world had shattered. I had hit my bottom.

"Hey, you, okay? You look pale," said Michael.

"Yes," I answered, "It must just be the drug in my system."

"Okay, don't worry, just one stop for food, and then we will be home."

I said nothing as I struggled to keep my composure. Instead, I started to think—about my first mistake—because considering took me on an unprepared journey. Review led my mind to wander from the day we met to the following days. How much bullshit had I happily swallowed? And how much of it had I known to be the lie it was? But denied that truth to myself. Why had I lied to myself to stay with him when I had known I needed to push away?

Had I been too afraid to be alone to accept the truth and walk away? So did I just close my eyes and turn a blind mind and deaf ear to all the lies. Because what?

I wanted to believe the person I was with was priceless, and it hurt to realize that, at least to them, I had a price. How much was I worth to him? How much am I worth to me? Will these events teach me to place no one on a pedestal higher than myself, or was I doomed to repeat these same events, hoping for a different outcome?

What was my price? I thought if I had one, was there an actual monetary value? We pulled into the carryout parking lot and waited in the car. A woman, maybe two years younger than me, came out two minutes later to retrieve my check card. I handed it to her. Michael watched her leave, contemplating what she looked like underneath her khaki pants.

He caught me looking at him, looking at her, and gave me a smile.

"Isn't this great? You'll be done by Monday, so I can help you move out next week!"

I looked at him, rolled my eyes, and kept the words inside my mouth that were fighting to come out. Why had I never realized what an asshole he was? What was wrong with me? Were the drugs we did together that kept me passive because he was egotistical and insolent? The same girl brought out the food. I signed the receipt and gave her a copy. Michael gave her his most winning smile before he drove off. I went back to my writing.

I was distressed when Sean broke up with me; he was my first boyfriend, and it still hurt though I hadn't been in love with him. After all, he had been the first black guy to accept me and not make fun of me for being Haitian. At least, that is what I had thought at the time, but now I knew it was more than that; it was the fact that he was a bad boy who skipped school, a good-looking guy that had wanted me while everybody else wanted him.

I had gained esteem and recognition from being his girl, a position I did not get on my own, like the white boy Eric in middle school. Being with him helped me get noticed and pay attention when I would have been ignored.

So as soon as we were over, I went back into my shell of not caring for the opposite sex's company, only sharing myself with Dean Koontz, Lee, Lenard, and sometimes Jeanne. Gloria tried to be there for me but made things worse, so I usually left her and Ken alone.

Summer school ended as it had begun, and life went on without me much involved, as usual. Then, finally, freshman year started. William H. Turner Technical Arts High School was as unique in its 'students' content as its long name. Unlike my junior high school, this school's intellectuals surpassed their prejudice. At least, that's what I thought until three months into the school year when I became infatuated with this Costa Rican guy who looked exactly like Keanu Reeves.

José was an inch shorter than I, with dark hair and eyes. His smile was as beautiful as any that Keanu ever gave on the big screen, if not better, and his shyness surpassed mine, so much so that I was intrigued into becoming friends with him in our physical education class. He made me laugh in a way that when I was with him, nothing seemed to matter. He was so much more innocent than I was, and he was so sincere. He melted my heart and made me want to spend all my time around him. He was the sweetest person I had ever had the pleasure of having in my life, then and now.

He had a gift for me every day and never asked for or accepted anything from me in return. The gifts were mostly computer printouts of Mickey Mouse and Minnie kissing, or hugging or holding hands, with captions that said things like "I love you," or "I can't stand being away from you," or "Would you be mine always," but at that age, those small tokens were all I needed from him.

I was still not allowed to go out on a date. Therefore, to see me outside of school since we only had one class together, José would ride his bike five miles to my house just to watch TV by my *side. And sometimes, if my mother felt extremely generous and normal, she would take me to his house to hang out. Of course, only after she made sure someone was there with us. His mom did not speak English; my Spanish could have used some work, but I never thought of it. She was always cordial and very friendly in my presence. I would have never believed that she had a problem with my ethnicity.*

Not until the arguments started between her and him. José was her youngest child. Her baby boy and she made it clear to him that she would prefer that he date a girl from a Spanish background. He never told me the arguments were about me, and she would ensure I could not hear what she was saying. Until one day, I called him, she must have placed her palm over the mouthpiece to muffle her words, but they were still apparent.

My Spanish was not excellent, but I could still understand when someone spoke badly of me. Finally, I confronted him, he apologized, and we moved forward. I did not want to lose him over something so stupid.

As our freshman year ended, things between José and me became more physical. I was the last remaining person in my group of friends who was still a virgin, and José was one, too. Of course, we were in no hurry to do it, but I was interested in knowing what all the fuss was about.

It was July 4th, and my mother took my brothers and sister to buy fireworks to play with that night. José and I found ourselves alone for the first time. We started kissing in my room. Little did I know that day would be when the loss of my sexual innocence would occur, and maybe that is when I started confusing love and lust. Though I seriously doubt that our feelings were real, even if they were not true love.

He touched me, kissed me, and held me. He made me feel sensations I never knew existed but had always somehow known were buried beneath the surface. It was not like the heat of your first sip of Haitian rum when it ran down your throat into your belly to explode into a kiss that enveloped your whole body. No, not like that. I was already familiar with that feeling. Instead, this new sensation teased you into thinking you may eventually discover this incredible experience's true mysteries.

It promised you completion beyond belief. It hinted that once you had achieved what it could give you, you would never need anything else, and you wanted it to be true so bad that you believed the tingling in your body to be a revelation of all of life's greatest mysteries. But it never revealed anything. Nope, no mystery was solved, no awakening of your senses. Instead, you're left there, inches from complete.

Wanting, waiting, and wondering where that feeling had gone. At least, that is what I felt like after my first time. He was exhausted. Breathing hard out of his mouth and nose. I lay on my side, staring at nothing for a while. Then, finally, I told him we should get dressed before my mom got home.

Chapter XIX

C'est Mon Vie

We went upstairs and sat down to eat. Food cartons were spread out throughout the coffee table. I went to the fridge, grabbed one of the beers I bought last night, and brought him water. I said nothing to him, and he said nothing to me for almost a whole fifteen minutes.

"So, how's the apartment hunting?" Michael said while finishing the last of the fajitas.

"Fine," I said

No longer having any appetite for the more than half of my food that remained in the plastic containers, which was slowly turning the same 65 degrees that Michael liked to keep the apartment, I closed the container, stood up, and went to the kitchen to put the rest of my food in the refrigerator.

"Well, that's good. Tell me if I can do anything to help you with it."

I bit my lip hard, almost enough to draw blood, trying to keep quiet in the kitchen. Then, deciding that maybe a change in the conversation's focus would be best for me, I continued.

"So now that you're free and clear, what are you planning on doing?" I returned to the table and started clearing the rest of the stuff.

"I want to concentrate on myself for a while. You know, get a new car and buy a house."

I stopped dead in my tracks, stunned by those words coming out of his mouth. I pivoted on my heels halfway to the kitchen to look at him. Did he really think that what had just come out of his mouth was his idea, or did he realize that he was just playing Pinky to his friend's Brain?

Two months ago, Max, Michael's best friend, had ended a four-year relationship with his girlfriend, not that I blamed him; she had been a controlling, somewhat psychotic bitch, for lack of better words. So, he quit smoking, joined the gym, and started hanging out more with us at the local clubs, something Max's girlfriend had denied him. Soon after, Michael tried to quit smoking and joined the gym, which he hardly went to, so I guess that made me the girlfriend factor he had to eliminate.

Wow, he was an even bigger idiot than I thought. I reconsidered what I was about to do and closed my mouth before a stray house fly found the comforts of laying eggs inside me appealing and returned on my route to the kitchen.

He got up, left the living area, and went to the bathroom. I guessed to take a dump or something until I heard the shower come on. I wondered if I stood at the kitchen sink with the cold water running would it affect the temperature in the shower. Maybe so much so that he would get a cold and be unable to sleep.

God, I was terrible at this if that was the only thing I could think of to hurt him. Thanking God for at least being pretty, if not wise, I moved to the couch to watch TV and kill more of the few brain cells I had left. "Law & Order - S.V.U" was on, so I stopped my channel surfing to watch. When the show went to a commercial, Michael walked out of the shower and toward me.

"What do you think?" He held up two vertically striped shirts, both long sleeves but with different color schemes.

"The one with the dark blue accent," I said while I pointed to the one in his left hand since he was colorblind. "Where are you going?" I sat on the couch, waiting for an answer since he started walking back into the bedroom.

"Oh, remember I told you that Rick from work plays in a band. So, I'm going to hear him play."

Inhale, exhale. Had I really believed that crap about him caring for me all weekend? Maybe I had not believed it, but I had hoped he meant it.

"I thought you would take care of me all weekend." I snapped back before I realized I was talking, hitting myself on the forehead with the palm of my hand for the stupid mistake.

He came out of the bedroom wearing the shirt I had indicated, straight black jeans, and black Timberland loafers.

"Babe, it'll only be a couple of hours, and then I'm yours," he said while rubbing the gel into his hair. Then, he turned around and walked into the bathroom to check himself under better lighting.

"Hey, what about the painkillers the doctor prescribed for me? You said you would get those."

"I will, on my way back. It's only a little after four, and Walgreens doesn't close until nine. So, I think you should be fine till then."

I didn't say anything. I wanted to argue that I might be in severe pain when he came back, but I didn't feel like showing him that I needed him in any way, shape, or form. So, I just closed my mouth.

He kissed my forehead, smelling freshly scrubbed and cologne, and walked out the apartment's front door.

I looked at my watch, astonished that he was right about the time. What had been going on with time the last couple of days? I looked up from my watch to the TV. To find that I had lost a whole segment of the show. It was again on a commercial. I reached inside my purse on the end table next to me. Retrieving my phone, I saw I had no missed calls, something that I only recently got used to since moving to Sarasota. I dialed Edwin's home number. He picked up the phone on the second ring.

"Cologne," he said, in the singsong way I was used to from him.

"Wow, you're home early. I wasn't really expecting you. I just wanted to leave a message asking how you are since I had not heard from you in a long time," I admitted.

"How many new recruits did you scare out of wanting to serve the Stars and

Stripes today?" I asked, speaking of his job at the armed forces recruiting station.

He laughed. I loved his laugh. It was hearty and robust and came from a deep place inside of him. It was the kind of infectious laughter. There was a way that his eyes squinted at the corners, and he licked his lips when he laughed.

I could imagine him lying on the one oversized king-size black couch in his living room, cream carpet going grey from lack of care, an African Grey parrot inside a six-feet cage to the far right of the television in front of him, feathers molting and slowly accumulating on the living room floor below the cage.

I shook my head with a smile on my face. That damn bird did not like me and often scared the crap out of me. When I used to hang out over there, it would move toward me, beak opened like it was ready to strike.

"Yes, the future generations of military recruits are safe to enter service now that I'm home. So, how is the redneck? I mean, the redneck town you're in," he said.

"Nice Freudian slip, ass," I said, laughing.

"Thank you, I'm here all day."

"Anyway, you shouldn't be talking. You're from Idaho. I could call you a redneck, too."

"Ohio."

"Whatever, you're a redneck, too." I finished sticking my tongue out at him through the phone.

"I was only born there. I grew up in Florida."

"Whatever, what are you doing?"

"Laying here, getting ready to cook dinner."

Oh, and the man could cook. I mean, he was not a five-star cook or anything. However, when all the men you know can only make sandwiches to sustain him. Themselves, Edwin, being able to make an actual meal was terrific. So, what had I thought when I had dropped him like a hot potato with some lame excuse that I owed it to myself to see if I could make things work between Mike and me?

"What are you cooking?"

"Spaghetti."

"Spaghetti?"

"Yes, spaghetti. What's wrong with that?"

"Nothing, I'm just surprised. What happened to the usual?"

By the usual, I meant a two-and-a-half-pound T-bone steak or four twelve-ounce pork chops, either served over a bed of steaming white rice. What can you say, at six-feet-seven and two-hundred and twenty-five pounds, the man could eat. However, I was not complaining. It did his body good, and so did being in the Navy.

Edwin was perhaps one of the better-looking men in my circle of friends, though when I used the term 'friend' with Edwin, it was in the loosest of meanings.

"I have physical training all next week, so I'm trying to eat light right now," he said.

He was talking, but I was only half-listening to him, lost in my thoughts of his piercing blue-green eyes. Sometimes favoring either color depending on what mood he was in. And how he looked in his all-white Navy formal; I used to feel like I was floating on air being escorted around by him, everyone looking at us with envy.

Jesus! How did I not see till now how every guy I had ever dated I had only done so for the attention I got when I was with them?

"Hey, am I talking to myself here?"

"Nah, I'm here. You were saying something about P.T." I snapped out of my train of thought.

"So yeah, I'm on a sort of crash diet."

I laughed.

"What's so funny?"

I heard the scrunching of the leather against his skin. A low grunt escaped his lips. I visualized him moving past the computer desk with the two monitors he used for online gaming and into the kitchen. In my mind's eye, I could see him walking around the kitchen of his apartment, the phone in one hand, the other turning off the faucet. In front of him was the kitchen counter, which he had turned into a bar. At least twenty different liquor bottles were lined up, waiting for the best the armed forces had to offer to come over and start a poker game.

"Spaghetti is not much of a diet food, and I just can't imagine you on a diet," I finally admitted.

"Neither can I, plus it's lighter than steak. So, the way I figure it, for every pound I lose, it's a pound I don't have to run five miles carrying. So why are you calling anyway?"

I had not really expected him to ask the reason for my call. However, Edwin was never one to be subtle with his thoughts. The day he had asked me to be his girl, he had been very forward with it. No stuttering, no hesitation. When I told him no, I was not ready. I was still torn about Michael. He had blatantly told me Mike was an idiot, and I should have never let him back in my life. How I wish I had listened now.

"I don't know. I guess I just wanted to hear the voice of a friend."

"If you move back, you would never have that problem. All your friends would always be around."

"Yeah, I know."

"So, what's stopping you?"

"Pride," I said before I realized what was coming out of my mouth.

Pride, which, above all, was the valid reason behind me staying here. My own selfish pride. I would live in a purgatory of my own making because I was too proud to admit that I was wrong and this whole thing was a mistake.

"Yeah, well, good people have died for their stupid pride. Do not let yourself be one of them. I got to go. Call me later, okay?"

I agreed and hung up. Then, I sat on the couch, putting the phone on the table.

Would I let my pride be the death of me? Was I that stupid? I thought I knew how stupid I was. I had suffered dearly for it in the past. Would I allow myself to continue to suffer for it in the future? Pen to paper, I continued my journey into the past, hoping that it would help me find answers to my future . . .

Things between José and his mother had escalated by the beginning of the sophomore year. Now she didn't really care whether I heard her dislike of me. In fact, she went out of her way for me to know how she felt about me. However, we still loved each other very much. I could not take seeing him in pain. Their arguments became more heated, and I began spending more time crying than laughing. Finally, after hearing things from her that I was never meant to hear, I broke up with him a year into our relationship.

Love is a very educational thing. Love teaches you to be stronger, kinder, and more receptive to your fellow human being. However, it can also be a very masochistic bitch.

At twenty-four years old, sitting here writing this, my thoughts wandered back to the conversation Edwin and I had once before. It was after Mike, and I had first fallen apart, and we had just met. I felt much pain, and Edwin was very nonchalant about it. After a few drinks, I asked him if he had ever experienced love. Edwin simply answered that he had not. And, in turn, asked me how I knew it was love that I felt and not lust?

I did not know. And it made me wonder whether I should envy him or pity him for never knowing love.

I would have envied his immunity to love if it had been back then during my youth when I was still tender. But instead, I felt the complete pain of my loss. My tears would not subside, and I lay myself to sleep each night straight for a week with the dried tears of anguish clinging to my cheeks and sorrow in my heart.

The last quarter of my sophomore year was without joy or laughter. Winter turned to spring with little change in the tropical weather to mark its transformation in sweet southern

Florida, except for maybe a ten-degree fluctuation on the skin, the thermostat, and fewer beach days.

José and I still spoke to each other in passing, but the love we once shared was undying and a sharp pain whenever we were close. Our friends knew and tried their hardest to lighten each other's situation. We smiled, laughed, and secretly stole sideway glances at each other. How I longed to be wrapped in his arms once more. A week before the summer that marked the end of sophomore year and the beginning of the junior year, José cornered me alone in an empty hall.

I saw him walking toward me and turned to walk the other way. Along the walls of Turner Hall, the paint changed from teal to orange marking the change in academy-grouped classes. His hand reached out and grabbed my arm. I flinched, my breath caught in my throat, and my heart began to race with speeds I imagine only an Olympic sprinter would know. I had frozen in place without realizing it. At least, not until I felt his breath against my neck. And the warmth of his body pressing against the back of mine.

He whispered in my ear that we needed to talk. The smell of peppermint and the heat from his body sent a shiver down my spine. My knees went weak, yet I still could not move.

He walked around and faced me. I turned my head, and with a strength I did not know he possessed, he gently pushed me against the orange-painted wall. Standing there, I tried desperately not to look into his uncommonly beautiful brown eyes. Then, tilting my head gently toward him, he slowly walked into me. The kiss was hard, his lip soft against my own.

I never wanted him to stop. However, he did. In addition, he said the most devastating thing that my ears had ever heard, far harsher than the vile words that my mother shrieked at me in an abnormal attempt to raise the perfect offspring. Even viler than what my mother said, my grandmother screamed and did to her in her own twisted method of discipline.

"I'm transferring to another school," he said. "I can't go to this school anymore. I love you too much. This is killing me inside."

Kissing me once more, he walked off. I did not know what direction he took or how long I lingered there with tears running down my face, still feeling the warmth of his kiss, registering the words he spoke, wanting to vanish into nothingness.

Love is a very educational thing. Love can teach you how to endure the loss of your love.

Men Are Not The Problem

Continues in...
Volume III

About the author

Luna Charles, is a Haitian-American writer who has authored numerous books, articles, and essays. Besides being an accomplished author, Luna is also a dedicated student of Theology, Metaphysics, and Philosophy. As a mother of two lovely girls, Luna has spent most of her life in South Florida.